DEMANDING REDEMPTION

FORBIDDEN SERIES #5

TRACY LORRAINE

Andy and Amelia

CHAPTER ONE

I SUCK IN A DEEP BREATH, trying to rid myself of the frustration the drive here created. I had planned to give Erica the perfect date night, to show her exactly how it should be done, but I failed at the first hurdle by getting stuck in London rush hour traffic that was only made worse by the roadworks closing two of the lanes.

I grip the wheel until my knuckles turn white as I prepare for the rest of my night and hope it might go a little more smoothly than my day's been. I've had back-to-back meetings in which all I seemed to have done is firefight issues on our jobs.

Pushing that to the back of my mind, I try to focus on Erica. Imagining what she might be wearing and how she might have done her hair makes me forget about work.

I hadn't intended on taking anyone home the night

I spotted her in The Avenue, but one look and I was hooked. I'd never experienced anything like it, but my need for her was all-consuming. It had been a while since I'd been with anyone, but there was no way that I was leaving without her.

Life hadn't been great in the lead-up to that night, but the prospect of a new job did have a little hope creeping in that things were about to turn around for me. I'd spent the weeks before that night trying to give my life some kind of purpose. Everything I'd known up until that point had come to a painful end. I'd instigated it all, but that didn't mean the huge upheaval after years of stability wasn't a shock to the system. All of a sudden, I found myself alone with no one caring what I did or where I went. I'd thought it was going to be freeing, but, in reality, after so many years of the exact opposite it was a little unsettling. I imagined I was going to revisit my youth, have the kind of fun I'd missed out on all those years ago, but after only a couple of nights out with a few of my single friends, I knew that kind of life wasn't for me. I needed something different, and it wasn't until her red hair and sinful curves caught my eye that I discovered what it was.

I thought one night without any expectations or promises might break the spell she'd cast over me, but it only cemented my need for something a little more serious. I didn't want to be giving anyone a ring in the near future or anything crazy like that, but the prospect of getting to know someone new, some dates and some fun, excited me.

Then, she turned out to be even more that I could have imagined. The morning I walked into the office of my new job and found her bent over, dropping files into a box, I knew that I'd do whatever it took to make her mine.

"Good evening, Trey. Long time no see," Mark, the maître de, says as I approach his desk.

"Good to see you," I respond with a chuckle, taking his hand when he offers it.

I have a permanent reservation here once a month on a Friday night. It was a tradition that I started many, many years ago, and it just stuck.

"You're a lucky guy tonight. The woman sitting at your table is a beauty." Something bubbles up in my stomach at the knowledge that he's checked Erica out. I know he's no threat, but still, I hate the idea of another man's eyes on what's mine.

He winks at me before ushering me in. "I know the way." Clasping my hand on his shoulder, I nod, smile, then head into the restaurant.

As always, every table is full. The wait list to get a table here is weeks long, if you're lucky. There are only a few people that I know of who have permanent reservations, and that's only because we're friends with a member of staff or have more money than sense. Thankfully, one of my oldest friends just so happens to be the head chef here.

Excitement flutters in my belly as I round the corner. Lifting my eyes, I scan the room, desperate to find her. Sadly, the moment my gaze lands on my usual table, the feelings I was expecting don't happen. My mouth doesn't water, my body doesn't ache with need, and my cock doesn't swell to be inside her. Instead, the only thing I feel is fury.

Red hot fury.

"Where is she?" My voice is low and menacing, but she doesn't so much as flinch.

"Your little *friend* has left. You really are having a mid-life crisis, aren't you? Filing for divorce. Sleeping with a girl young enough to be your daughter. How do you think this looks, Trey?"

"I don't give a shit about how it looks, and I don't owe you an explanation for any of it. We're done, Sarah. Why are you even here?"

"I've waited long enough, but after the stunts you've been playing the past few weeks, I thought it was time I came and rescued you from yourself."

"Rescued me?" I ask, incredulously.

"Credit where credit's due, Trey, she was beautiful. I can understand why you've been pulling out all the stops and ditching your family to impress her. Fancy hotels, giant bouquets of flowers. Dinner at *our* restaurant."

"This isn't *our* restaurant. It might have been where we came to enjoy each other's company a long time ago, but that hasn't been the case for years, Sarah. What I do now has nothing to do with you."

"No? Then why do I still see all your credit card statements when I log onto our joint bank account? Why is that I still have your email account attached to my phone so I know what you're up to?"

Her words make my blood boil.

"I told you to remove all that."

She shrugs, and it's like a red rag to a bull. Reaching out, I grab her arm and pull her from the chair. "What did you say to her?" I'd never hurt a woman, but if I were ever to change my mind then it would be now. My fingers dig into her upper arms and something inside me settles as her eyes widen in fear.

This woman's known me since I was a child, and the fact that she seems scared of me tells me exactly where her head's at right now. She refused to accept my decision to leave all those weeks ago, so I'm not sure what I expected when she discovered I was seeing someone else. It's one of the reasons I hadn't told her about Erica. I had every intention of doing so once I knew things were serious, but I've got bigger things to worry about than what my ex-wife thinks.

"I just introduced myself." A small smile of victory curls her lips. "It seems you've been about as honest with your little friend as you've been with me."

My heart pounds and my head spins as I try to put myself in Erica's shoes. I promised her I wouldn't let her down, yet the one thing about my past that I've been keeping a secret was just thrust in her face.

"Stop calling her that. She's not just some quick thing. I really li—"

An unamused laugh falls from her lips. "Please don't tell me that you really believe she feels anything for you. Girls that age aren't thinking about forever, about their future. You're just a toy to her, probably to show off to her friends."

Stepping closer, I stare down at her, my eyes boring into hers. "Don't pretend you know anything about her. About us." She wants to laugh again, but she stops herself when my eyes narrow. "We're done, Sarah, so if you would kindly sign the papers I know you've received, we can move on with our lives." Stepping back, I turn to leave. "And remove my email from your phone," I call over my shoulder before walking straight past Mark, who stares at me with his mouth gaping open, clearly wondering what the hell's going on.

"I had no idea she was here," he calls, but his words

don't stop my escape. There's only one person I need to speak to right now, and I'm determined to make her hear me out.

My head tells me she won't be there, but my body's on auto-pilot as I drive towards our building.

I don't remember the journey. My head is too focused on how the hell I'm meant to get her to hear me out. I've no idea what Sarah might have said to her or how bad she's made the situation out to be because, in reality, I've done nothing wrong. Sarah and I are over and have been for a long time. I'm not cheating on her, and Erica is most definitely not the other woman.

She's the *only* woman, as far as I'm concerned.

Sarah will always be a part of my life. That's not something that's ever previously concerned me, because I never expected her to act the way she did tonight. I knew she wasn't happy with our separation, but I never expected her to meddle when I tried to move on.

Slamming my foot down on the brake, I pull the car to an abrupt stop, blocking three parking spaces. Ignoring it, I rush from the car and up towards her flat.

"Erica?" I call, slamming my fist down on her door. "Erica, open up."

My voice echoes down the stairwell, but it doesn't stop me continuing. *If* she's inside, she's not going to be able to ignore me.

After a good few minutes, I stop banging and rest my head on my forearm against the door.

"Erica, please. If you're in there, just open up. Let me explain. Please." My voice sounds pathetic even to my own ears. I'm almost embarrassed of the weak mess of a man she's turned me into, but it only serves to prove how much I need her. I don't deserve a woman like her, I know that. She deserves to be a man's first love, to be his first everything. I can't give her that, but that doesn't mean I'm letting her go anytime soon.

Dragging in a few deep breaths, I try to get my head on straight. If she's not here, where would be the first place she'd run to?

Her sister.

Pushing myself from her door, I make my way back downstairs. I fight the disappointment that threatens at not finding her. I knew deep down that she wouldn't come here. It would be too easy. She'd be expecting me.

"What the fuck, man?" some guy who is clearly one of our neighbours shouts, gesturing to my car that's half parked in his space.

"Sorry, emergency."

"Just move it," he barks, clearly having about as good a Friday as I am.

With a curt nod in his direction, I jump in my car and pull out of our small car park. Thankfully, the drive to Erica's sister's is short, the traffic finally starting to let up a little.

The beep of my car locking behind me cuts through the silence on her street. Stopping at her front door, I take a breath and try to compose myself. Once I'm a little calmer, I lift my hand to knock gently.

It's only seconds before a light comes on and a shadow falls under the door. The moment it starts to open, I push my palm against it and shove it wider, stepping into the small hallway at the same time.

"What the hell?" Sam asks, her panicked eyes flying over me. It's the first time I've seen her, and I'm immediately struck with how similar she is to Erica. Her hair's brown opposed to Erica's fiery red, but everything else—their green eyes, build, height—is so familiar yet so different at the same time. There's no denying they're sisters.

"Is she here?" Just like Erica, Sam doesn't back down from my demanding tone.

"No, she's not. What have you done?" I hesitate. Sam puts her hands on her hips and narrows her eyes on me. "If you've hurt her, I'll—"

"Our meal was intercepted and she ran off."

"Intercepted?"

"Not important right now. Where is she? Erica?" I shout into the flat, convinced that her sister is probably covering for her.

"She's really not here. I haven't spoken to her today."

Ignoring her, I step forward into her living room and then each room I find. All the while, Sam stands in the hallway, watching me with a gobsmacked look on her face.

When I come up empty behind the final door I find, I walk back towards her.

"Happy now?"

"Do I look fucking happy?"

"No, you look like a man who's just fucked up big time."

Her small body blocks the front door, stopping my escape. My lips twitch at her attempt to make me explain.

"I need to find her, not be standing here talking to you. Excuse me." My hands land on her tiny waist and I lift her out of my way.

"If you've hurt her, I'll kill you," she calls out as I head back towards my car. I can't help the small amused chuckle that falls from my lips.

"I'd like to see you try." Looking back over my shoulder before I drop into my car, I expect to find a pissed expression on her face, but what I find is one of pride.

"What?" I ask, confused.

"Just go and sort your shit out. I hope she gives you hell."

Rolling my eyes, I drop down and slam the door behind me. Was that some kind of approval? She has no idea what happened tonight, yet she seems to be weirdly happy about it all.

My only other option is Lauren and Ben, so I set off in their direction.

"TREY?" Ben asks, pulling the door open with a beer in hand.

"Have you seen Erica?" I try not to allow concern to filter into my voice, but with the way his eyebrows rise, I'm not sure I'm successful.

"No. Why?" Accusation drips from his words. I don't need to tell him that I've fucked everything up. He knows, and he's already in full-on protective mode. Taking a step forward, his shoulders widen and his chest lifts. It's exactly the way he looked when he caged me in at the restaurant a few weeks ago after I'd fucked her in the bathroom. Back then, I was glad she had someone like Ben looking out for her. Now I've screwed up, I'm not feeling so good about the fact that he could quite easily keep her from me and end my new job in one foul swoop.

"There's been a bit of a misunderstanding." I cringe as the words leave my mouth, but I don't really feel like standing here and explaining everything to my boss, who also just happens to be one of my girl's closest friends.

"Baby, who is it?" Lauren calls seconds before she also appears and tucks herself into Ben's side. The sight of them together makes my heart twist. They have such an easy relationship, like they've literally found the other half of themselves. "Trey? I thought you were taking Erica out for a meal tonight."

"Yeah, things didn't quite go as planned. Have you seen her? Heard from her?"

"Is she okay?" Her sudden over the top concern is enough to make me think they know more than they're letting on.

"Look, if she's here, please just let me talk to her. It's not like it seemed."

"She's not here," Ben says just as Lauren opens her mouth to respond.

"I just need to explain. Please."

Lauren looks over her shoulder at Ben, and I can't help feeling like I'm getting somewhere... until Ben shakes his head at her.

"If we hear from her, we'll pass on that you're looking for her. But if you can't find her, it's probably because she doesn't want to be found."

"But—"

"I told you not to hurt her," he growls. "We'll always be on her side."

"But it's not—"

"I'm sorry, Trey." Lauren's eyes are full of sympathy as Ben pulls her back into the house and swings the door shut on me.

"Fuck," I shout into the silence of their driveway.

Now what?

CHAPTER TWO

STUMBLING OUT OF THE AVENUE, I stare down the street at my car, knowing that I can't get in it. I came here in the hope that it might have been her place to escape to, but the only thing I found was a vintage bottle of whiskey that was sitting on the top shelf behind the bar.

I've never felt so lost. I have zero fucking clue what I'm meant to do now to try to fix things. I can't even fucking find her, let alone make her listen to me.

I somehow manage to find the strength to flag down a taxi, and, after slurring my address at him, I'm thrown back against the seat as he takes off across town.

The world outside passes by as one big blur, but I don't see any of it. All I can see is her. Her green eyes that darken, hungry with need every time she turns them on me. The delicious lines of her body that make my mouth water to even think about. How hot and tight her pussy is every time I slide balls deep inside her.

My cock swells as I rest my head back and replay all our times together. I'd never experienced sex like that until her. It's fucking mind-blowing. Erica is meant to be a part of my life, and I have to figure out a way to prove to her that I'm still worthy.

FORGOING THE STAIRS, I head straight for the lift. The temptation to kick her door down is going to be too fucking high if I so much as catch a glance at it.

Attempting to shut down the thoughts of her flat being right beneath my feet, I fumble with my key and eventually fall into my living room. I just about manage to catch myself when the door I was leaning on for support flies open with a quick turn of the key.

Shrugging off my jacket, I allow it to fall to the floor before tugging at the buttons running down the front of my shirt. I manage a couple before my frustration gets too much and I pull until the satisfying sound of them pinging around on the wooden floor fills my ears.

Reaching into one of my kitchen cupboards, I pull out a half-empty bottle of whiskey and twist the cap.

Foregoing a glass, I tip the bottle to my lips and swallow a generous measure.

I pull my phone from my pocket and fall down onto the sofa. The phone calls, voicemails and texts I've left for her have all gone unanswered, but that doesn't mean I don't try again.

Putting the phone to my ear, I wait for it to ring, but this time it just goes straight to voicemail.

"Motherfucker," I slur, throwing my phone down onto the other end of the sofa before lifting the bottle back to my lips.

WHEN I WAKE the following day, it's with one serious kink in my neck, a throbbing head, and the rain pounding against the windows.

"Fucking hell," I groan, trying to drag my body from the sofa but only managing to roll off, hitting the wooden floor with a bang.

I must land on the bottle, because the sound of glass echoes through the room as it rolls off somewhere. The memory of how much I must have consumed last night causes my head to drop back against the floor. The room around me spins, telling me that I'm no use to anyone today.

I somehow manage to pull myself to my hands and

knees and embark on the seemingly monumental challenge of getting my arse to my bedroom.

I've no clue how long it takes, but I do know that I pathetically stop for a rest a few times along the way, hoping it'll help stop my stomach churning and my head from spinning. I sigh the second my body sinks into the memory foam mattress, and I'm almost instantly out like a light.

SATURDAY IS MOSTLY A BLUR. I stumble from my bed to use the bathroom and grab some food before falling face-first once again into my pillow. I know that self-pity isn't a good look on me, but I'm struggling to pull myself out of it. I feel utterly useless. I've no idea where she is, and my calls still go directly to voicemail, leaving me with no way of explaining.

It's not until the sun starts streaming in on Sunday morning that I begin to feel a little bit like myself once again. With the raging hangover cleared, I jump from the bed and grab my running kit with a new lease for life. I'm going to fix this, and she will listen to me. I won't give her the chance not to.

My feet pound the pavement as sweat starts to cover my brow. My muscles pull in the exact way I need, and it helps relieve some of the tension that's been keeping my body locked up tight.

I'd hoped that inspiration would hit while I was out, but as I push the key into the lock, I've still no fucking idea what I'm going to do. Pulling off my t-shirt, I wipe the sweat from my face and throw it into the wash basket as I start up the coffee machine.

I call her phone again, but I'm greeted by the automated voice on the other end that I'm getting fairly familiar with. Next, I try Ben in the hope that they might have heard something, but his short, sharp answers don't help at all and all but confirm my suspicions that he knows more than he's letting on.

I wonder about going back to her sister's house when another thought hits me. My parents are too far away for a heart-to-heart, but I know someone who'll probably be able to talk some sense into me right now.

I have a quick shower before pulling on a fresh pair of joggers and t-shirt, grab my keys, and head out. Not wanting to turn up empty-handed, I stop at a bakery on the way and pick up some fresh pastries.

"Trey?" Chris asks, his eyes still clouded with sleep when he pulls his front door open. "Do you know what time it is, son?"

"I'm sorry. I didn't know where else to turn."

Chris, or Uncle Chris, as I've always known him, is one of my dad's oldest friends. Even after my parents both moved away, Chris has always kept in touch. I might be a grown-arse man, but he still likes to keep an eye on me, probably to report back to my parents.

"Come on in."

He pulls the door wider and I follow him down towards his kitchen.

"Morning, Trey," Jenny, Ben's mum sings, sounding and looking much more awake than Chris.

"Morning. I bought pastries."

"Oh, you can come again," she laughs, going for plates.

Chris disappears to change while Jenny makes us all coffee. When he reappears, he walks straight over to her, wraps his arm around her waist and drops a kiss to the top of her head. The move makes my heart twist painfully in my chest. They're both proof that second chances are possible, and it gives me a little hope that things will be okay.

"I'll leave you boys to it," Jenny says with a plate and steaming mug in hand. "I'll be in the snug if you need me."

I thank her; she can obviously tell that I'm not just here for an everyday visit.

"What's up then, boy?"

"I screwed up," I admit.

"Go on," he mumbles around a mouthful of pastry.

"I've been seeing Erica." His eyebrows lift for me

to continue, so he clearly knows who I'm talking about. "I didn't tell her about Sarah, and she intercepted our date Friday night. Erica's run fuck only knows where, and she won't answer her phone. Ben and Lauren obviously know something but won't tell me. I don't know what to do."

"Why didn't you tell her? It's not like you're still together. I'm sure she would really have appreciated your honesty."

"I just wanted everything to be perfect. I didn't want to bring my past into our possible future, and I had no idea how she'd cope with the knowledge that it's not just me she's going to have to accept into her life."

"And how well did that work out?"

"Fabulous, thanks for asking."

"Trey," he says, placing his mug down, his serious eyes finding mine. "How much do you know about Erica?"

"Uh..." I really want to be able to say a lot—after the time we've spent together, it really should be more than it is. "Not all that much." Almost every time I've asked her a question about herself or her past, I can physically see her shutters coming down. I know she's been hurt so her hesitance to open up is understanding, but how much she's kept from me has frustrated me more than I'm willing to admit. "She told me about her dad and how he treated her like she was nothing. I know a few little things about her ex and that she had something to do with Nick, but everyone's been pretty tight-lipped about the whole thing."

"Her ex upped and left her in a shit ton of debt. She'd saved for years to buy her flat and she was on the verge of losing it." Pride swells in my chest for what she's managed to achieve. Sadly, it's pushed aside as anger that someone she trusted could have taken that away from her. "If you know about her dad, then I'm sure you appreciate that her upbringing and teen years weren't all that great, so a stable home is important to her."

"Makes sense." I nod.

"That girl's been through so much. She's trusted all the wrong people, and they've walked all over her. It's why she's kept you at arm's length. She's afraid it'll happen all over again. She's used to men taking advantage when she's weak; it's exactly what Nick did."

"What did he do?" Leaning forward on my seat, I hope that he's going to shine a little more light on the situation everyone in the office has skirted around for weeks. The company's issues due to the old boss are impossible to miss; it was ultimately the reason for my employment and the very reason our office is crawling with auditors and final demands for payments.

"He blackmailed her into keeping his dirty secrets. And then he made her one of them."

"He slept with her?" I spit, the disgust evident in my voice.

"Nick was...an arsehole. He took exactly what he wanted and manipulated every situation exactly as he wanted it. Erica was drowning, and he knew it. He used that against her."

"Motherfucker." My heart pounds and my teeth grind as I discover what I had somewhat suspected but wished I was wrong to be true.

Erica needs someone who's going to fight like hell to prove they're trustworthy, not someone who's going to have lied from the get-go. That's exactly what she's expecting, and she needs to learn that not every man wants to take something from her.

"What the fuck am I meant to do?"

"Tell her the truth, beg for forgiveness, and spend the rest of your life proving she can trust you."

"What if she won't listen?"

"Make her."

"Fucking hell."

"Nothing worth fighting for is easy, Trey, but thanks to the events of her past, this fight is going to be even harder. Is she worth it?"

CHRIS' words ring in my ear the whole drive back home. There was only one answer to that question.

Yes, she's worth it. She's worth it a million times over.

I just need the chance to prove it.

Taking the stairs two at a time, I hesitate at her floor. Something tells me that she still won't be there, but I can't risk not finding out.

Rapping my knuckles against the door, my heart jumps into my chest when I hear movement inside. The sound of a female voice is enough to have me on the verge of breaking the fucking door down to get to her. It's not until the voices are right on the other side that I realise my mistake. Whoever the woman is, she's not Erica.

My shoulders slump just as Joe opens the door, revealing him and the woman, who is Erica's opposite in every way possible. My eyes widen when another guy joins them and he and the woman go to leave. Stepping aside, the woman nods at me, a small smile twitching her lips in greeting before I watch as the pair entwine their hands and descend the stairs.

Turning back to Joe, I raise both my brows at him.

"I know what you're thinking, and yeah, it was a fucking epic night."

Shaking my head, I focus on what I'm really here for. "She's not here, is she?"

"No, she's not. I don't fucking blame her, either. You're married."

"Separated and waiting for her to sign the damn divorce papers."

He lets out a long breath as he studies me. He must be happy with whatever he finds, because he soon steps aside and invites me in.

"Coffee?" he asks over his shoulder as I follow him to the kitchen.

"Black, no sugar."

"Sweet enough, huh?"

"I didn't mean to deceive her."

"I believe you."

"Really?" I wasn't expecting him to invite me in let alone be on my side here.

"Yeah. I genuinely think you care about Erica, and I believe that you wouldn't intentionally hurt her. But —" I groan at the emphasis he puts on that one word, "—you have hurt her. You lied to her after promising that you weren't like all the others. Although she'd never admit it, she trusted you. She was willing to give you the benefit of the doubt after telling herself that she'd never let another man close to her again, and you've just proved her right that men can't be trusted."

"She trusts you."

"She doesn't trust me, and she's right not to. I'm just as big as a fuck-up as the men of her past, but it's different with us. I'm not in love with her, and we have no romantic future together."

His words confuse me. To the outside world and his colleagues, Joe is this muscular, tattooed guy that, although obviously younger than the majority, oozes confidence and demands respect. What he just said is the polar opposite of that, and it makes me wonder who the man standing in front of me really is.

"I have zero advice when it comes to women and relationships, and if I were to give you some, I'd advise you take it with a pinch of salt. But you've gotta fight for her if you want her. Erica is a stubborn, independent bitch at the best of times, but after what you've just done, her walls are going to be higher and stronger than before. She's been hurt too much."

Every time someone tells me how often Erica has been hurt, that someone has broken her trust, my heart aches that little bit more and my anger and need to avenge her grows. She is hands-down the most incredible woman I've ever met, and the fact she's been used time and time again has fury unfurling in my stomach. My need to protect her and keep her safe explodes through my veins.

"Tell me where she is? I can't set about proving anything until I find her."

"Nah, I'm not getting involved. She'd kick my arse if I told you."

I lift a brow, glancing down at his body. The hours he spends at the gym are obvious: he's got the biggest arms I think I've ever seen in real life. There's no way my little redhead could kick his anything. "I think I'd pay to see that."

"She's stronger than you'd believe."

"Oh, I believe that. I just want to see it."

"Erica's..." he pauses, a small smile appearing on his lips. "Incredible. Her strength is amazing, her ability to bounce back is out of this world, but at some point she's going to break, and you'd better make damn fucking sure you're not the cause of it."

I nod, the emotion of how far he'd go to protect her clogging my throat. Erica might have had some bad people in her past, but I really hope she appreciates the incredible people she has around her now. She's created her own little family who will protect her no matter the cost.

"Can I use your bathroom?"

"Knock yourself out."

I do what I need to do and intend on heading straight to Joe for another shot at getting the information I need out of him, but when I step from the small room, her bedroom calls to me. Slipping down the hallway, I push the handle down and step inside. Her scent hits me immediately, like a bat to the chest. Lifting my hand, I rub at the ache and walk over to her bed. Just being here makes me feel closer to her, which is crazy because she could be miles away.

Lying down on her bed, I allow her essence to surround me and think back to how good everything was before I fucked up just like she was expecting me to do. I knew I should have told her about my previous life from the get-go, but I was so swept away by her that I never found the right time.

Pulling my phone from my pocket, my heart drops at seeing no replies to any of my previous messages or calls. Opening the camera, I stretch my arm out as far as it will go and snap a selfie of myself on her bed.

> Trey: I miss having you beside me. Please come back and hear me out. It's not how it seems. Please?

It's delivered immediately and, to my amazement, those two little ticks turn blue for the first time in days. My heart thunders in my chest and the phone in my hand trembles as I wait to see if she's going to reply.

Nothing happens. The little bouncing dots I was hoping to see never appear.

CHAPTER THREE

JOE NEVER GAVE up her hiding place. Although it's frustrating as fuck, it fills me with happiness that she can trust him, even if he believes he's totally untrustworthy.

When I wake on Monday morning, excitement and anticipation fill my veins. She can hide all she wants over the weekend, but she's got a job that she loves and people relying on her, so I know I'm going to see her this morning.

I don't get nervous, but when I pull up outside our office I'm pretty sure the sick feeling in the pit of my stomach and the sweating of my palms is exactly that.

Feeling ridiculous that a woman can have this kind of effect on me, I suck in a deep breath and throw my door open.

It might only be Ben in the office when I walk in but already the atmosphere is heavy.

"Trey? Get in here."

His voice is deep with an angry edge, so I don't hesitate to follow orders, which isn't usually something I'm all that happy about—but if this has anything to do with Erica, I'm all ears.

"What's up, boss?" I try to keep my tone light but one look at his face and my shoulders tense. I'm not going to like what he's about to say, that much is obvious.

"Look," he barks, twisting his screen around violently so I can see it.

Dear Ben,

It's with huge regret that I am giving you my resignation, effective immediately. Johnson & Sons hasn't just been a job for me, it's been my family, and I will miss it more than I could possibly explain. I was welcomed with loving arms and, for the most part, it's continued until this day. I've made incredible friends who I hope will still be there as I embark on the next chapter of my life—hell knows I'm going to need you. I am contactable via email if there is anything that needs my attention. I will help you out in any way I can until you are able to find my replacement, but I will not be visiting the office.

With regret and love,
Erica Wilde

My eyes burn as emotion fills me. Stumbling back from her words that cut right down to my soul, I fall over one of the chairs and only just about catch myself.

"Motherfucker," I roar. My fist finds the freshly plastered stud wall and smashes right through it.

My knuckles burn on contact, but I welcome it. It's better than the pain radiating from my chest right about now. Dragging some much needed air into my lungs, I pull my hand back and assess the damage.

"You've got a meeting in twenty minutes. Get your shit together. You can worry about fixing that when you get back." His words are harsh. He's placing every single bit of blame for this on my shoulders, as he well should, but fuck this hurts. I've never been such a big disappointment to people I cared about. It's a feeling I'd rather not get too used to.

I wince as warm water trickles over my cut and tender knuckles, but it's only small compared to the pain I deserve for what I've caused. The water immediately turns red, and I watch transfixed as it swirls in the bottom of the basin before disappearing down the waste.

The realisation that in Erica's eyes I'm no different to any of the men of her past makes my breathing falter. I knew my omission of the truth had hurt her, but for her to hand her notice in? A familiar ache reappears in my chest. I hurt her more than I even realised.

Lauren's just walking into the office as I leave. Concern fills her eyes as we pass, but she doesn't say anything, just watches me get in my car and drive away.

I can't help feeling like she wants to help me. The look in her eyes is different from everyone else's. They all want to keep me as far away from Erica as possible, which is exactly as she's instructed, I'm sure. But Lauren is different. Maybe it has to do with everything she and Ben went through to get where they are now. I've no idea, but she wants to help, I can feel it. I just need to get her alone.

ON TUESDAY MORNING, I get my first opportunity to talk to Lauren. She's in the kitchen making coffee, Ben's out at a meeting, and everyone else is engrossed in whatever they're doing.

It's now or never.

Pushing the door closed behind me to cut off eavesdroppers, I walk over to where she's looking out of the window, waiting for the kettle to boil.

"I need your help."

Her head snaps around and her eyes widen when she finds me right behind her. "Shit, I didn't even hear you come in."

"Please. I need to know where she is. I need to talk to her."

"I can't, Trey. I won't break her trust."

"I need her. I need her to hear me out. I promise you it's not as bad as it looks."

"Your wife turned up for your date. It looks pretty bad."

"She's not my wife. Well...technically she is until she agrees to sign the papers. We've been over—this isn't important right now. Erica's the only one I need to explain this to. Please, I know you know where she is, just tell me."

I don't mean to, but the more I start begging, the closer I get and the more I cage her in. I'm so desperate to get the answers that I'll do anything—including intimidating the boss, it seems.

"I can't." Emotion starts to swim in Lauren's eyes, and I know she's about to break.

"I can sort all this out, I promise. I just need her to listen."

"Enough." A large hand lands on my shoulder and forcefully pulls me backwards. "Back off."

My back hits the counter as Ben cages me in. We're

similar heights, but he's got a fair bit more muscle than I have, so I wouldn't back myself if something were to kick off. Plus he has the obvious age advantage on his side. His eyes bore into mine, his face hard, his muscles pulled tight like he's about to throw a punch any minute.

"Ben, it's fine."

"He had you pinned in the fucking corner," he seethes, his cold eyes never leaving mine.

"I wasn't pinned. It was nothing. Just leave it." Out of the corner of my eye, I see her wrap her small hands around his arm, and he visibly relaxes.

"Go fucking near her again, and you won't be stepping foot back into this office."

"Ben!" Lauren gasps, her eyes wide with shock.

"Just tell me where she is. I know you both know." I make one last attempt to get what I need.

The couple look at each other. Ben's head shakes ever so slightly, and Lauren accepts it.

"Erica trusted us not to tell you, and I'm sorry, but our loyalties lie with her. You're going to have to figure this one out yourself."

Both of them leave the room and, once I'm alone, I spin around, rest my palms on the counter and hang my head in defeat.

I spend the rest of the day silently getting on with work at my desk, desperately trying not to glance up at her empty one. I can't look anywhere in this place without seeing her, and it's driving me to distraction. I've already fucked up one price I had to submit, and I've ordered the wrong kit to one of our jobs. I'm a fucking liability right now, and I can't see it getting better anytime soon.

As the day comes to a close, Lauren appears from her and Ben's office and sits in Erica's chair. I watch as she blows out a breath and looks at the framed picture on Erica's desk of the two of them, Joe, and another girl I don't know.

Sadness radiates from her in waves as she starts collecting up Erica's stuff and placing it into two empty boxes. I note that she's putting work related stuff into one and her personal possessions into the second. The work box is placed on a shelf while she walks out with the other after having a quick chat with Ben.

Without putting too much thought into it, I close my laptop, grab my stuff and follow her out. I have no idea if she spots me. I keep my head down and pretend I'm done for the day as I climb into my car and start the engine. I allow her to go on a little ahead, but I keep a close eye on the direction she takes and trail after her from a distance.

I'm so focused on not losing her that I have no idea where we are when she eventually pulls the car to a stop. Thankfully, I manage to find a space a little down the street, and I prepare to get out to continue following if necessary, but when I watch her walk into a hairdresser's without the box in hand, I sit back and relax. This plan is really going to go to shit if I have to sit here and wait while she has her fucking hair done.

My phone rings, and, after pulling it from my pocket to check that it's not Erica, I throw it into the console and focus on not missing Lauren's departure. Thankfully, after only a few minutes, she's back out. She casts her eyes down the street before stepping from the shop, and I duck in panic. But she returns to her car and her indicator comes on as she goes to pull away. I follow moments later.

I trail her through a residential area, and my hopes start to rise that, at any moment, she could pull over and reveal where Erica's hiding, but other than stopping for a couple of red lights she just continues.

When she does eventually indicate and pull over, I almost miss it because of the distance between us. I end up passing her and parking on the other side of the road as she gets out and goes into an Indian food shop.

Waiting for her to appear again takes longer this time, and when she does, she has a bagful of stuff. My stomach rumbles loudly as I imagine what she might be cooking later with all of that, reminding me that I didn't have any lunch earlier.

She sets off once again, and I fall into place a few cars behind her.

The cat and mouse act soon starts to get old when she stops two more times, once at a chemist and again at a corner shop not all that far from her home. Every single time, she gets back in the car and heads off again.

The next time she stops and walks into a shop, I pay a little more attention as the mannequins in the windows show off a selection of sexy lingerie and stickers advertising that the latest Rabbit is now in stock. My balls ache as I imagine how Erica would look wearing what's in the window; better than those plastic dolls, that's for sure. It feels like a lifetime ago I was last inside her. My need to plunge my cock deep inside her body is beginning to get the better of me. My cock swells, and I rest my head back, closing my eyes just for a few seconds as I allow myself to revisit my memories of what it's like to be with her. To feel the softness of her curves under my hands, to suck her sweet skin into my mouth and listen to her moan and beg for more.

Banging beside me scares the shit out of me. Jumping a mile out of my seat, I turn to see who's interrupted my little erotic trip down memory lane.

"Fucking hell," I groan when I find a very smug looking Lauren staring back at me. Lowering the window, I swear her smile only gets wider.

"Credit where credit's due, Trey. I really thought

you'd get bored before I did, but I've got shit to be doing. This little tour of London has been fun and all, but I kinda need to get home and cook dinner."

My chin drops at her words. She was playing me?

"Oh, don't look so surprised. I saw you pull out from the office after me and then every time I looked in my mirror, there you were. I get that you want to see her, Trey. I really do understand, but she's asked me not to tell you where she is, so I'm not going to lead you right to her door."

I narrow my eyes at her and she laughs.

She lets out a sigh and looks at me, her eyes full of sympathy. "Use your head a little. Think outside the box. You know her better than she thinks you do. Figure it out. Prove to her that, no matter what, you can find her. That you need her just that badly."

CHAPTER FOUR

THIS WEEK'S BEEN HELL, but, as I pull up on the driveway of my old home, I know things are about to look up, if only for a few hours.

It still feels alien knocking on my own front door, but I guess that's what happens when you walk away from your own life.

"Wow, I didn't think you'd show your face this morning."

"Are they ready?"

"No. I assumed you'd be too busy chasing skirt."

"Shut the fuck up, Sarah. When have I ever just not turned up?"

"You've not been here the past two weekends."

"Which I told you in advance about." I shake my head as she stands her ground, keeping her foot behind the door so it'll only open a few inches.

"Girls," I call loudly enough to fill the house. "You ready?"

"Two minutes, Dad," Ella calls as Sofia's feet start pounding down the stairs.

"Dad," she wails, practically pushing Sarah aside so she can throw her arms around my waist.

"Hey, baby. I missed you."

"Where have you been? You were meant to take us out last weekend."

"I know, I'm just trying to settle into my new place and my new job."

Sarah scoffs but thankfully decides to leave us to it. "Make sure they're back by seven. Ella's got a sleepover at a friend's."

"Sure thing."

Keeping Sofia tucked into my side, we wait as Ella appears from upstairs with her coat on, ready to go.

"Dad, you okay?" she asks the second her eyes land on me.

"Yeah, of course. Ready to have some fun?" In truth, one look at her and I was struck with a wave of emotions so strong I struggled to fight them back down. My babies are growing up too quickly, and now I'm no longer living with them I'm missing out on so much. It was the main reason I stayed here as long as I did. My two girls are my life. I'd do anything for them, but keeping up appearances that we were a happy family could only last so long. At twelve and fourteen, they aren't babies anymore. They're young women, and I couldn't be prouder of the adults they're becoming.

With them either side of me, we walk out to my car.

"What are we doing?"

"Theme park?"

"Yesss," Sofia squeals happily while Ella has a slightly more composed reaction.

"SO, HOW'S SCHOOL?" I ask Ella who called shotgun and took the front seat, much to Sofia's frustration.

"It's good. Same as usual. Not enough PE lessons and way too much math."

I chuckle. It's the same response every time I ask. With Ella staring down at her phone, I look in the mirror at my youngest daughter. "How about you, Sof?"

Sofia's reply is much more animated as she dives into every detail of school life, barely letting up for air before we reach the theme park. I know everything about her classes, friends, and the birthday party she's going to soon. She's practically bouncing with excitement as we queue for tickets, unlike Ella who's much more placid about what the day holds. It's not unusual for her to be the quieter, more thoughtful one of the two of them, but I can't help but wonder if there's more going on in her head.

We both follow Sofia around and go on all the rides she wants to go on. It warms my heart, seeing her so happy, but that doesn't mean I forget about the quieter one of the two who happily follows her around and smiles at all the right times. She's much more focused on whomever she's texting than on what's going on around her.

"Can we go on the log flume?" Sofia squeals when we walk towards it.

"No way. I spent way too long on my make-up this morning to get wet."

"Dad?"

"How about you go, and we'll watch."

She pouts but after a few seconds agrees to the plan and happily bounces off, while Ella and I find a bench to sit and watch.

"What's up, kiddo?"

"Have you got a new girlfriend?"

"Uh..." I wasn't expecting this. "What's your mum said?"

"Nothing. I overheard her on the phone talking to Auntie Sue."

"Oh right. You shouldn't eavesdrop, baby."

"I wasn't, I just walked to the kitchen and she said it. She said she's young enough to be your daughter."

Rubbing my palm down my face, I try to figure out what to say for the best. "She's not young enough to be my daughter, although she is a little younger than me."

She lets out a disappointed sigh. "You're really not coming back home, are you?"

"I'm so sorry, El. Things between me and your mum haven't been right for years. I needed to get out."

"I get it, Dad. I just miss you."

"I miss you too, more than you could ever know." I wrap my arm around her, pull her into my side and kiss the top of her head.

"Sometimes I just need a hug from you."

I hold her a little tighter as a ball of emotion clogs my throat. I know how important it is for teenagers to have both parents around—hell, everyone needs their parents around, no matter how old they are.

Fuck.

"Dad, are you okay?" Ella asks when I noticeably tense against her.

"Yeah, yeah. I'm fine." In reality, I've just realised how to find Erica, and I'm frustrated because I didn't think of it sooner. She told me herself that every Sunday she and her sister visit their mum. Tomorrow morning, I'll know exactly where she'll be.

Feeling my shoulders loosen for the first time in days, a small smile twitches at my lips.

"Oh my god, that was epic!" Sofia screeches as she comes running over, dripping wet from the ride. "Give me a hug, sis."

"Do not touch me," Ella fumes, standing from the bench and backing away.

"That's enough, you two. Shall we get out of here and get dinner?"

"Yes, I'm starving," Sofia complains, wringing out her hair.

"On second thought, we'd better wait until you've dried off a little."

CHAPTER FIVE

SPENDING the day with my girls was exactly what I needed, and not just because Ella was the inspiration to figure out where I'd find Erica.

I'm up bright and early the next morning, pacing my living room and hoping the minutes will tick around quicker so I can see her. It's been over a week and I'm missing her like crazy. It's enough to tell me that the words I said to Chris last weekend were true and that she is very much worth it.

I don't leave the flat until I know she'll already be there. I might want to surprise her, but I don't want to ruin her visit. When I got back last night, I Googled the care home and discovered it specialises in dementia patients. I've no idea how old Erica's mum might be, but I was surprised to read that, seeing as Erica is only twenty-six.

Gripping the wheel painfully tight once I've pulled the car to a stop outside the home at the opposite end of the car park to what I recognise as Sam's car, I replay everything I need to say to Erica in my head. I already know that she's going to do anything possible not to listen to me. After a week of hiding, she's not likely to hear anything I've got to say willingly, so I need a plan.

Sucking in a deep breath, I throw the door open and step out. My legs feel like jelly as I head towards reception. The place looks exactly as I expected. Neutral, minimalist and quiet. Finding a seat in a dark corner, I sit and wait. I've no idea how long they'll stay —I guess it depends on how their mum is.

My leg bounces and my heart pounds the longer I sit there. Every time I hear female voices, my heart jumps into my throat, but it's never them.

I begin to think that maybe they're not here and the car I assumed was Erica's sister's in the car park was actually someone else's. Just as I'm starting to think about leaving and giving it up as a failed attempt, two soft voices filter down to me.

"So, how are you really doing? The morning sickness getting any better?"

That's not them. It can't be.

Blowing out a frustrated breath, I wait for the women to appear, knowing it's not going to be her. But they don't get that close before my stomach twists to the point I worry I might be about to throw up on my feet.

"No, it's not subsiding at all. I swear I actually feel worse each day."

I don't need to see her to know that is her voice. Erica's...Erica's *pregnant*? My hands tremble as I fight to drag in the air I need.

I should probably stick with my plan to make my presence known, but when Erica and her sister walk around the corner and my eyes land on her for the first time in a week, my body turns to stone.

She looks as beautiful as the last time I saw her, but even I can't miss the slight greyish tone to her skin, making the words I just overheard seem even more real.

She's fucking pregnant?

Those words are still on repeat in my head as I watch them both get into the car I suspected was Sam's, but thankfully they don't pull out straight away. It gives me a chance to bolt from the reception and into my own car so I can follow them. I need to know where she's going so I can talk to her. If what I just overheard is true, then it's more important than ever that she hears me out.

I trail them from a distance, hoping like hell that I'm doing a better job of it than I did with Lauren. When they pull into a car park outside a pub, I follow and hope that I manage to discreetly park a little farther in the shadows.

They both exit the car and walk towards the pub, so I assume I was successful. I'd like to think that, if they suspected something, they'd come over. I'm not sure about Sam, but I know for a fact that Erica wouldn't be able to ignore me if she knew I was watching.

Waiting for them to reappear is the longest hour of my life as I sit there and think about the possibility of being a dad for a third time and going back to having a baby. It was so long ago that my girls depended on me like that that...I think I've forgotten how to do it all.

A year or so after Sofia was born, Sarah started begging me for a third. I always refused. I think I knew back then that something wasn't quite right, although it would be years before I'd come to terms with it. Having another baby was never an option, as far as I was concerned. We had our two perfect girls, and that was more than enough for me. But what about now? Could I have another baby all these years later? What would my girls think of that? Would they accept it? Hell, I have no idea if they'll even accept Erica, yet let alone a sibling.

Sitting back in my seat, I wait for them to be inside the car once again before starting my engine and attempting to secretly follow them.

When they pull up outside Sam's flat, I breathe a sigh of relief that they're not going to give me the run around like Lauren did. I park a little down the street and allow them to go inside while I try to figure out what the fuck to do.

Needing to hear a rational voice before I decide if I'm going to go storming into Sam's house and confront her, I grab my phone and call Chris.

"Trey, how's everything going?"

"It could be better."

"What's happened now? Have you found Erica yet?"

"Yeah, I've found her. I've also discovered that this thing between us is more complicated than I thought."

"Why?"

"I think she's pregnant." The words feel unnatural falling from my lips, but I don't panic the way I would have expected if someone would have told me this was going to happen.

"Okay. So does that change things?"

"I've no idea," I say, honestly.

"Is she still worth it?"

"Yes." The answer is out of my mouth almost before he asks the question. I don't even need to think about it.

"So what are you waiting for? If you know where

she is, go get your girl and stop wasting time talking to me."

"Fuck."

"Just go," he says with a laugh before hanging up on me.

Blowing out a long breath, I push myself from the car and make my way towards the flat.

Waiting for someone to answer the door after ringing the bell are the most nerve-wracking few seconds of my life. I'm not sure whether I'm excited or relieved when it's Sam who pulls the door open. Not wanting to give her a chance to slam it in my face, I put my foot inside.

"I know she's here. I need to talk to her."

"Hi, nice to see you again," she says with a sickly sweet voice. "I wondered how long you were planning on sitting out there. Oh, don't look so shocked. You'll never make a secret agent." My mouth drops open that I've once again been caught. "She has no idea, mind you," she adds.

"Are you going to let me in?"

"I'm gonna let you in, but you should know that if this goes badly, I'm going to claim you forced your way in."

"Whatever," I mutter as she stands aside and lets me past.

"Kitchen," she calls, pointing down the hallway.

"Who is...fuck," Erica says, her eyes widening when she looks up and finds me in the doorway. "What the hell are you doing here?"

"Coming to pick up what's mine."

"I'm not a fucking object, Trey. I've got nothing to say to you, so I suggest you leave the way you came."

"Erica, please. It's not as bad as it seems."

"What, you didn't lie to me about being married?"

"Can we do this in private?"

"No, we're not doing this at all. You ruined whatever we had the moment you lied to me. You're just as bad as all the others. Actually, no...you're worse, because you promised. You promised you were different and that you'd never hurt me like they did." Seeing tears fill her eyes and her chin tremble as she fights to stay strong almost breaks me. I never wanted to hurt her, and I was desperate to keep my promise to her. I know I should have told her long before she was forced to discover the truth, and that's totally my fault, but I refuse to lose her over it.

"Erica, please. There's so much you don't know."

"Exactly, which is why my answer is no. We're done, Trey." Her determined stare meets mine—until I drop the bombshell that she really isn't expecting and they widen in shock.

"We're not. Especially not while you're pregnant."

Her face pales, her eyes fill with tears, and her head shakes in disbelief.

"How'd you know?" she whispers.

"Let's get out of here and we can talk." Her shoulders are still tense as she sits and considers my suggestion.

Eventually, she lets out a sigh and says, "Fine," before pushing the chair out behind her and getting up.

I stand and watch as she gives her sister a hug goodbye. "Just hear him out, yeah?" I don't think I'm meant to hear it, but Sam doesn't whisper quietly enough.

"We'll see," Erica says before turning toward me. "Well, come on then." She sounds far from happy about it, but at least she's willing.

Stepping up to her, I place my hand in the small of her back and hate when she flinches away from me.

"I said I'd listen. I didn't agree to anything else," she hisses, and my heart drops. It looks like I've got an even bigger fight on my hands than I expected.

I hold the car door open for her and wait patiently as she gets in, but at no point does she look at me or say anything. The entire journey is the same: she stares out of the window, totally ignoring my existence.

Not wanting to go back to either of our flats, I head towards the park we walked around the other Sunday after our night at the hotel. It feels like a million years ago now. She was overly emotional that weekend; I guess it all makes sense now I know she's pregnant.

Finding a space on the edge of the park, I pull the car to a stop and get out. Thankfully, she gets out and meets me on the pavement. My arm aches to reach for her, to entwine our fingers together, but I know it would be a bad move, so I attempt to ignore it as I take a step forward, hoping that we can find a bench and that she'll hear me out.

The park is pretty quiet for a sunny winter afternoon. There are a few joggers and dog walkers on the paths and just a couple of kids kicking a ball and laughing in the distance. The sight of them sets me off thinking about what the future might hold for Erica and me. Could we be here in a few years kicking a ball around, or am I about to become a dad to another child I won't have full access to?

Blowing out a slow breath, I try not to get ahead of myself. She's yet to say anything, so there's no point in jumping to conclusions.

Erica follows me over to an empty bench and sits down beside me. When she doesn't say anything, I do.

"It was never my intention not to tell you about Sarah, about my past. Things were just a little intense, and my focus was on you and our possible future. I'd spent the past few months, years really, trying to figure out how to best move on with my life, and it was finally happening." She doesn't respond, but I do catch her glancing over at me from the corner of her eye, so I continue. "Things had been over between us long before I moved out. We'd been together since we were fourteen, and I don't think either of us really wanted to admit that we'd grown apart. But we had. We were no longer the people we once were, and we both wanted different things."

"How?" It's the first word she's spoken in a long time, and it starts to give me a little hope that she's really hearing what I'm saying.

"I wanted to get out and try new things before we got too old. I wanted to travel, do all the things the two of us wanted when we were younger and couldn't afford to. But she was happy at home doing her thing. I started to resent her, and I knew it was time to call it quits before we ended up hurting each other. I moved out about three months ago, although our relationship was long over. I quit my job and went travelling. I needed to find myself. Shit, I sound like a teenager or something, but I had no idea who I really was without her. I'd spent all of my adult life with her by my side, but I couldn't do it to myself any longer. I needed more than she could offer me."

"Okay," she breathes, before she falls silent once again. The sound of the cars behind us filters through the trees and mixes with the bird song up above. The cool air gently blows past us, but neither of us seem to notice. We're too lost in our own world that could be about to crash down around our feet. "Do you have anything else to tell me? Because now would be a really good time." Her voice is weak and broken. I hate that I'm the one to have caused that. I promised never to hurt her, but I fear I may have caused more pain than any before me if her dejection right now is anything to go by.

"Sarah and I have two kids." Saying that out loud feels like a huge load lifting from my shoulders.

Her eyes burn into the side of my head and I turn towards her, my breath catching at the exhausted and devastated look on her face.

"Jesus, Trey." She slumps back against the bench, and I panic.

"I'm so sorry. I never meant to lie to you, I was just so swept away by you and starting a new job, and then as the days went on and we became more serious, I just didn't know how to say it."

Placing a protective hand on her belly, I'm reminded of what she's also been hiding.

"I'm not the only one with secrets though, am I?"

"Do not even try to compare the two situations. You actively hid your family, your past, from me for weeks. I'd only just discovered the truth and I had every intention of telling you that night, only your wife interrupted. How did she even know I'd be there?"

"We used to go there regularly," I admit with a wince.

"So I was just stepping into her place in your life?"

"No, no way. It really is my favourite restaurant—that has nothing to do with her. The head chef is an old friend of mine and the food's incredible."

"I wouldn't know, I didn't get the chance to find out," she snaps.

"Where do we go from here?" I ask, beginning to feel like we're just going around in circles.

"I..." she starts but blows out a long breath instead of finishing her sentence. "Do you want more kids, Trey?"

My silence must clue her in as to where my head's at. "Fuck, you don't, do you?"

"I didn't think I did, no."

"Fucking hell." Standing, Erica stares down at me. She wants me to tell her I didn't mean it, but I promised her, and myself, that I would be totally honest.

"I wasn't expecting this. It was the last thing I thought I'd overhear while I was sitting in the care home waiting room for you to appear."

"You were at Park View?"

"Yeah, I figured I'd find you there."

"Huh, smart move," she mutters to herself like she hadn't considered I'd think of it. "It doesn't really matter how long you've known. People's first reaction to things is usually correct, and if you're saying now that you don't want any more kids, that's how you feel." Seeing her hand on her belly once again guts me.

"No, I'm not saying—"

"That's enough." She puts her other hand up to stop me. "I can't listen to any more right now. I need you to take me home."

"Erica, please. I—"

"No, Trey. Take me home, or I'll call a taxi." She starts digging through her bag, and I panic that our time might be over.

"Okay, okay. Let's go."

Tension radiates from her as she turns her back on me slightly and stares out of the window. The drive to our building is the most painful journey of my life. Every inch of my body is begging to reach out and touch her, to do anything to make it all better, but I know I can't. I can't make it better, and I can't touch her.

"Where have you been all week? I've been going crazy."

"At a friend's."

"Are you planning on staying now?" I ask, nodding towards our building as I pull into the car park.

"I've no idea what I'm doing. I'm without a job, and I've no way of paying the mortgage, so..." she trails off, and I feel like the worst human being on the planet.

"Come back to work, Erica. I'll leave if I have to." She shrugs and reaches for the handle. "Wait. What now?"

"I don't know, Trey. I don't know anything right now."

"Can I see you again?"

"I'll call you."

"When?"

"I don't know." Her voice is getting harder and her words more clipped. I know I'm pissing her off, but I can't let her go, knowing I might not get another chance. "You hurt me, Trey. You lied to me about something so huge. I don't know if I'll ever be able to trust you again. I'll call you, but I don't know when, so I suggest you don't wait by the phone." With that, she jumps from the car and slams the door behind her.

"Fuck," I shout, slamming my palms down on the steering wheel. It must be louder than I expected, because just before she enters the building, she turns to look back at me and my heart damn near explodes in my chest.

CHAPTER SIX

THERE'S STILL no sign of Erica on Monday morning
at work, and I hear no mention of her appearing. I
meant what I said yesterday: I'd willingly hand my
notice in if it meant she'd come back. The last thing I
want is her worrying about how she's going to pay her
mortgage.

I spend most of the day out of the office, which is a
good thing because I'm not taunted by her empty desk
all day. I'm not so lucky on Tuesday, as I find my only
meeting rescheduled for later in the week. With a huge
pile of pricing to get through, I turn myself into the
corner of my desk and try to block out my
surroundings.

By the time lunch rolls around, I lose my
concentration and find myself staring longingly at
Erica's side of the room, wishing she'd come bouncing

from the kitchen with a mug in her hand at any moment.

Sensing someone beside me, I turn to find Lauren perching herself on my desk. Her eyes flit over my face, and there's concern written all over hers.

"Have you even slept?"

"Not really."

"She's okay." If her words are meant to make me feel better, they really miss the mark. How could she possibly be okay after everything?

"She's pregnant." I don't mean to say the words aloud, but they seem to just fall from my lips.

"I know," Lauren whispers. Reaching out, she places her hand on my shoulder. "How are you holding up?"

"I miss her. I just...I don't really know, to be honest."

"You've fallen in love with her, haven't you?"

My heart thunders in my chest as I realise that it's true. "Yeah, I think I have."

I didn't expect any of this. I thought I'd leave Sarah and embark on a new life as a single man. I never even considered that I'd find love again, especially not so soon, but it's not like I can do anything about it. Erica has completely stolen my heart. If only she'd give me the opportunity to win hers.

"Have you told her?"

"What do you think?" I ask with a sigh.

"I know I probably sound like a broken record, but you need to fight for her. Prove to her how you feel and don't give her the opportunity to forget you." The thought of Erica forgetting about what we had has a sharp pain shooting through my chest. Surely it's not possible?

"She won't listen to me. She won't even see me."

"You need to make her. I've heard from a very reliable source that you aren't one to lie back and take it. So get out there and figure out a way to get back into her life...into your *baby's* life."

"Fuck. I'm gonna be a dad again." Lauren smiles down at me warmly.

"You didn't hear it from me, but she's moved back home."

Lauren pushes away from the desk, leaving me to wonder what I'm meant to do with that information. Erica made it very clear that she'll contact me when she's ready. As much as I want to demand that she spends time with me so I can prove myself, I also respect her wish for time. That means I need to keep myself in her thoughts even when not there—although after everything and her pregnancy revelation, I can't imagine she's had much chance to forget me.

Pulling up the website I ordered her flowers from last time, I find the most expensive bunch they have to offer and quickly pay, this time sending them to her actual flat. I also organise for a tub of the ice cream she loved so much to be delivered. I've no idea how she feels about her pregnancy, so I hold back from sending anything maternity related. For all I know, she isn't going to keep it. My stomach twists painfully at the thought, and my mouth waters like I'm about to puke. No, if she's even considered not going through with it, she'd have told me, right? She wouldn't have been unknowingly placing her hand on her belly like she was already protecting the little one growing in there.

Unsure of what else I can do right now, I try to focus on what I *should* be doing, but every few minutes, my mind wanders. I think back to when Sarah was pregnant and the things she said made her life a little easier. Grabbing a Post-it note, I scribble a few things down, intending on buying them for Erica when I get a chance.

Once I've emailed off the price I'm working on, I give up and head out of the office with my laptop tucked under my arm, intending to do some more from home. At least in my flat I don't have to stare at her empty desk. *No, but you'll know she's beneath you,* a little voice says. I push it away and climb into my car.

I SPOT Joe's van pulling into our building's car park as I get out of my car and pull the couple of bags of shopping I stopped off for on the way home.

"Hard day?" I ask when he steps from his van with a large sigh.

"Yeah, you could say that. The job I'm on is a nightmare, fucking asbestos everywhere."

"You fancy going for a drink?"

He pauses at the front door and looks up, I assume considering his roommate who's hiding out upstairs. "Uh…"

"I know she's back, and I promise to do as she asks and stay away, for now. I could just really do with—" Thankfully, he cuts me off from having to admit that I need someone to talk to who knows her.

"Yeah, no worries. Let me shower and I'll come up to you when I'm ready."

It's almost an hour later when there's a knock at my door. I was starting to wonder if he'd stood me up.

"Sorry, Erica got chatting. Shit, I'm sorry." I tried to hide my reaction at hearing her name and knowing she's just downstairs, but I think I failed.

"It's fine. Let me grab my coat and we can go. The less time I'm in this building, the better."

"You moving?" Joe asks from behind me, looking down at the houses I'd printed out as potentials.

"I've no idea what the fuck I'm doing right now. I

rented this place as a temporary thing until I figured out what to do with my life."

He nods, but I sense he wants to ask more as he backs out of my flat, allowing me to lock up.

"Is the pub around the corner okay, or did you want to go somewhere more..."

"Somewhere more..." I prompt.

"Fancy?" he asks with a wince.

"You think I'm pretentious?"

"I don't really know you. I'm just going by the fancy suits and the expensive car. I don't really picture you in a London boozer."

I chuckle. "You're something else, you know that?"

"So I've been told," he says sadly. I'd ask more if it weren't for the closed-off expression on his face.

The pub is pretty packed, but I manage to find a table at the back while Joe heads to the bar for a couple of pints.

"So those houses you're looking at. They family homes?" he asks with a raised eyebrow, dropping into the seat beside me.

"Of course. I only printed them yesterday."

When he looks back up at me, his eyes have softened. "You're really serious about her, aren't you?"

"Yeah, I am."

"Baby an' all?"

"I'll take her however she'll allow me to have her." I cringe—the words sounded better in my head.

"She needs you to fight for her," he blurts out but quickly snaps his lips shut. "Shit, I promised her I wouldn't give you advice."

"I'm trying to honour her wishes and give her some space. She said she'd contact me, and I'm trying really fucking hard to allow her that."

"That must be fun." The smug smile on his face shows me how much he's enjoying my torment after hurting her. It's clear how strongly he feels for her and that he only wants the best for her.

"Listen, she'll kill me if she finds out I told you this, but..." He glances around as if he expects her to jump up and shout at him for even suggesting getting involved. "She'd never admit it, but she really wants a white knight to sweep her off her feet and rescue her from herself. She's telling you she needs space, but really, what she needs is you. Get in her face, show her that you can't live without her. Prove to her how important she is to you, how much you need her."

"So you're suggesting I break your door down and demand she listens?"

"Ambush her."

"What?"

"Catch her off-guard. She won't have her walls so high as she would if she's expecting you."

"Okaaay. So..." I'm not asking for suggestions by trailing off; I'm more trying to scheme up a way to do what he suggests, but he helpfully gives me the answer.

"Her sister's wedding is this weekend. It's at St.—"

"Margaret's Church followed by The Ivy. I know, I saw the invite last week."

"So..."

"So what?"

"Get one of your fancy arse suits out and surprise the shit out of her."

His words are on repeat in my mind the whole time we're in the pub and long after I fall asleep that night.

CHAPTER SEVEN

I'M AWAKE LONG before the sun rises on the morning of Samantha's wedding. I've been battling with what to do for the best ever since Joe brought it up.

Knowing Erica the way I do, I know that today is going to be a big deal for her. Her sister and her have a special kind of bond, and I'd hate to get in the middle of what should be a memorable day for both of them, but, in the end, my need for her gets too much. When I climb out of bed, I find my feet taking me towards my wardrobe to pull out a suit suitable for a wedding.

Erica told me little bits about today, so I know it's only an intimate ceremony with close friends and family. I already know my appearance will stand out like a sore thumb.

I'm ready hours before the ceremony is due to start,

but I'm too much of a nervous wreck to sit about waiting and allowing a million possibilities of what today might hold run around my head. Instead, I grab my car keys and head out.

I drive around the city before stopping at the end of Oxford Street so I can run into Selfridges to grab a wedding gift. If I'm gate crashing this thing, I can't exactly go empty-handed. I've no bloody clue what Samantha and her new husband might want, so I settle on a nice set of wine glasses. They're always a winner...right?

By the time I arrive at the church, the small congregation is already seated and awaiting the bridal party's arrival. I slip in at the back, totally unseen, and find myself a seat in the shadows. I might want to surprise Erica but I also don't want to freak her out at the most important part of today.

Everyone's chatter increases as the bride's arrival gets closer, and the groom, who's standing at the altar with his best man, becomes more and more nervous to the point that I start to wonder if he's going to puke on the stone floor.

When the music changes to announce their arrival, everyone around me turns to look at the doors while my heart jumps into my throat. It's been almost a week since I saw her and over two since she was in my arms. I'm more desperate than ever to get my hands on her.

Time seems to stand still as I wait for her to appear. Everyone's faces light up, so I know they're right there in the doorway.

I close my eyes and suck in a deep breath. When I look back up, there she is, standing beside her sister and looking more gorgeous than I've ever seen.

My heart hammers in my chest and my temperature soars just from looking at her profile. I can only imagine how she'll affect me when she turns her green eyes on me.

It only takes me a second to realise what's different about her: the fiery red hair I'm used to has gone, replaced by a more natural brown. It's almost all up in an intricate hairdo, leaving just a few loose bits hanging down her neck. She's wearing a copper strapless dress that fits her like a second skin, and my fingers twitch for the opportunity to peel it from her body.

Sam moves toward her soon-to-be husband, Erica takes a step, but something makes her turn her head. It's like she somehow knows I'm here. Her eyes immediately find mine. They widen in shock, and her skin pales as our connection holds.

Sam moves again but soon realises that her sister's frozen to the spot. Her eyes burn into my skin before her smile catches my eye and she nods in approval, giving Erica a firmer tug and almost dragging her up the aisle.

I pay no attention as the ceremony begins. The sounds of people sniffing and quiet sobs of happiness fill my ears, but at no point do I take my eyes from Erica.

She knows I'm watching her, because every few minutes she flicks her eyes my way just to make sure I'm still looking—although I'm sure she doesn't need to. She must be able to feel my heated stare.

Her chest heaves, and even with the distance I can see her swollen breasts threatening to escape from her dress. I drop my eyes over the smooth curve of her waist and hips as I start to wonder what she might have beneath. A tiny lace set of lingerie? A sexy corset maybe? I tell myself there and then that I'm not leaving this wedding until I've discovered the answer.

The service goes on forever. Every minute that passes, my need to get up and drag her out of the church becomes more and more intense. Watching her every movement from back here is torture.

I breathe a sigh of relief when the vicar announces that they're husband and wife, forgetting about the damn signing of the register.

Every muscle in my body is pulled so tight I swear the fucking things are going to snap by the time the wedding party heads back down the aisle and we're all able to stand and follow them out.

My intention is to make a beeline for Erica and

pull her aside. I've no clue if that's to tell her how I feel once again and how I'm not letting her go, or to beg forgiveness for turning up here in the first place. I guess only time will tell, but when I get outside, I find her surrounded by people and I realise I've got no chance. Dragging her away from them is a sure way to piss her off...if I haven't already.

I stand off to the side and, thankfully, no one comes up to talk to me. They must just think I'm some lonely old guy who either needed some company or has a weird love of weddings. A few guests glance over at me, but that's about it.

Just when I think I'm going to get my chance, the photographer announces that he'd like the bridal party to line up in front of the church so he can get some shots.

I'm on the verge of losing my shit after watching the guy take photo after photo of the same fucking thing when he calls that he only wants the bride and groom.

It's now or never.

I make my way through the guests who, like me, weren't invited to be part of the photos, and I wrap my hand around Erica's wrist just as she's about to move away from me.

"We need to talk."

She's silent as she trails behind me and around the side of the church so we have some privacy.

Pulling her so she has no choice but to stand in front of me, I stare down at her. Her make-up is flawless, but it doesn't quite hide the dark circles under her eyes or the redness tinting the edges. She's been sleeping just as badly as me. It's also a reminder of the morning sickness she must be suffering.

"How are you feeling?"

"Fine," she whispers, refusing to meet my eyes. It's the first time I've seen this shy side to her, and although it's not really her, it's endearing. I find myself stepping a little closer, desperate to feel her lips against mine. "You shouldn't be here. You weren't invited." Her anger starts to get the better of her, and her eyes find mine.

My breath catches as I stare down into their depths. "I know, but I couldn't wait any longer."

"This isn't the time nor the place, Trey. It's my sister's wedding. The last thing I need is you ruining it for me."

"That's not my intention. I just..." I let out a sigh, not wanting to ignite her anger because she's right, this isn't the time. "I need you."

"Yeah well, you should have thought about that before lying to me."

"Erica, please." I've no idea what I'm asking for,

but just the sound of my begging voice pisses me off.

"Trey," Sam sings, walking over with her giant dress pulled up around her ankles so it doesn't get muddy. "It's so nice to see you."

"Is it?" Erica mutters, and I can't help but smirk. I'm glad my little firecracker is still in there somewhere.

"I'm sorry I gatecrashed. I just needed to see this one."

Sam glances between the two of us like she's trying to decide what to do for the best. Erica's eyes narrow in warning, but Sam seems to ignore her.

"It's fine. I'd actually really love it if you'd stay. Our mum wasn't well enough to attend today, so we've got a spare place. What do you say?"

"What the hell are you doing?" Erica spits. "He can't stay."

"Of course he can. Plus, it'll give you both a little time together."

Erica fumes while Sam turns to me and winks. I know she far from approves of what I did, but it's good to know she's rooting for us.

"Thank you so much, I'd love to. And congratulations, by the way."

"Thank you. We're heading to The Ivy for our reception. We've arranged transport for everyone, but I'm assuming you drove. Erica," she says turning to her angry little sister, "why don't you go with him?"

"Don't you need me?" she asks through gritted teeth.

"Nope. I'll be fine. You should go with Trey."

I can feel the anger coming from Erica in waves as Sam smiles sweetly at both of us and walks back toward her waiting husband.

"Traitor," Erica calls out, making her shoulders shake with a laugh.

"Shall we?" I ask, holding my hand out to her. She looks down at it like it might burn her before she turns and storms off in the direction of the car park.

With a chuckle, I follow behind her, watching her arse sway in her fitted dress.

She doesn't say anything the whole way to the hotel. Instead, she stares out the window, her shoulders tense and her back twisted towards me. It's not exactly what I was hoping for, but at least she's in the same car as me.

I must be breaking her down, because, when I pull the car to a stop in the hotel's car park, she doesn't immediately throw the door open and run.

She lets out a huge sigh, and I can't fight back my words any longer.

"I miss you, sweetheart."

Sitting back, she glances over at me through her lashes. Tears fill her eyes, threatening to drop, but she fights them.

"Not good enough, Trey. I didn't want to trust you, but you didn't give me a choice. You made me promises, and, like an idiot, I believed them. I should have followed my gut. I should have learnt by now that no man can be trusted."

Scrubbing my hand over my face, I try to come up with something new to say. There are only so many times I can apologise. "It was my past, Erica. I was trying to focus on my—on *our*—future. I wasn't intentionally hiding it from you."

"But you didn't tell me. You had so many opportunities, but you just ignored it and allowed me to be ambushed."

"I know, I know. It's something that I'll regret forever. I never meant to hurt you, Erica, but I also can't live without you."

She sniffles, and my heart aches. I so badly want to pull her into my arms and make it all better.

"I need more, Trey. I can't keep being hurt like this." I open my mouth to respond, to tell her how I really feel, but she's too fast and I'm forced to watch her walk away and join the rest of the wedding party.

I debate whether I should just turn around and leave, but I figure that would be the easy way out. She said she needs more, so I turn the engine off.

I'm ready to give her everything.

CHAPTER EIGHT

SKIMMING my hand across the small of her back, my fingers wrap around her hip, pulling her into my body slightly. "Dance with me, sweetheart."

She stiffens, but, when she looks over her shoulder, her face is softer than I've seen it all day. Maybe it's the old romantic within that she fights like hell to keep buried, or maybe she's just fed up of fighting me—I've no idea, but when she steps away slightly and slips her hand into mine, everything in my world is suddenly right again.

I follow her lead and join the other couples who are already on the dance floor. Most of the night has consisted of fast-paced songs that have had Sam, Erica and their friends up on the dance floor. As fun as it's been to sit back in the shadows and watch as she wiggled her hips in time with the music and laughed like she had no cares in the world, we both knew that wasn't true. It's nice that's she's able to pretend, even if just for a few hours, but now the DJ has slowed the pace down a little and the silly dance moves and laugher has given way to a more romantic feel as couples of all ages sway and smile lovingly at each other.

I expected her to refuse my offer, so I make the most of pulling her body into mine once she comes to a stop on the edge of the dance floor. My hands come to rest on her lower back, teasingly close to her full arse. I press her tightly against me, reveling in the feeling of her soft curves against my hard planes. Her eyes flutter closed as our bodies move together.

She remembers.

Her hands slide up the lapels of my jacket and goosebumps prick my skin, wishing the fabric wasn't between us. As if she can't help herself once her arms are over my shoulders, her fingers start to tease the short hair at the nape of my neck. The sensation alone is enough to have my cock threatening to go half-mast. Having her this close, her sweet scent filling my nose, is a temptation I'm not sure I can resist.

"Have you had a good day telling everyone that you're my boyfriend?" she asks, her eyebrow lifting in amusement.

I shrug, a smile twitching my lips as I remember

the first person who came up and introduced themselves to me today. I greeted them like I had a fucking clue who they were and, when they asked who I was, I couldn't resist.

"You're mine. It's about time everyone knows it."

"Trey," she sighs, and my heart constricts, waiting for her to dismiss what's between us once again.

Dropping my head, I brush my lips against her ear. "I need you, and I know you need me too. Please allow me to make it up to you."

The longer I talk, the more her breathing increases. I know I'm getting to her.

"You can't tell me that you don't want me to take you to your hotel room right now and show you just how much I've missed you. You can feel that, right?" I thrust my hips, ensuring my now fully erect cock presses into her stomach.

A groan is her only response, but it's enough.

"You're remembering how good we are, aren't you? Remembering just how hard I make you come, how much you love following my demands. I can give you that right now, you've just got to ask, sweetheart."

She pulls back, her hungry, dark green eyes finding mine. She searches for a few seconds before they drop to my lips. It's all I need to know she's on board.

Reaching up, I pull her arms from around my

shoulders and take one of her hands in mine, leading her from the dancefloor.

She's silent behind me for a few seconds.

Stopping at the table where I know she dropped her bag, I pull her into me once again and stare deep into her eyes. "If you don't want this, you need to tell me now, because once I'm alone in a room with you, I can't promise I'll be able to stop."

Her neck ripples as she swallows and considers her next move, but much to my delight, she reaches out, grabs her bag and takes a step towards the exit.

"What are you waiting for?" she asks over her shoulder, and I rush to catch up with her.

We join another couple waiting for the lift. Thankfully, it arrives only seconds later and we all step inside.

"Four, please," Erica says politely when the lady asks what floor we need.

I move to stand behind her, wrap my arm around her waist and pull her back into me. With her high heels on, her arse lines up perfectly with my cock.

Brushing the tip of my nose against the sensitive skin of her neck, I smile as her body trembles in my arms.

"Do you reckon I could get you off before the doors open?"

Turning to look at me over her shoulder, she

doesn't give me a verbal answer. Instead, she licks her bottom lip before completely turning in my arms and pressing her lips to mine.

It's been two weeks since I've had her like this. Electricity shoots through my body the second our tongues tangle together, making my knees a little weak.

I lose all track of time as I focus on her kiss, and it's not until the couple occupying the enclosed space with us clear their throats that I look up and find the doors open on level four.

I nod at them appreciatively as I regretfully remove Erica from my lips and guide her from the lift.

"Have a good night," the guy calls as the sound of the woman's giggles filter down the hallway to us.

As much as I want to confirm that I intend to do just that, I keep my mouth shut and follow Erica as she makes her way to her room. I'm too focused on her and what's to come to worry about anyone else.

Her hand trembles as she lifts the key card to unlock the door. I wrap my own around her delicate one and hold it steady. Together, we swipe the card through the lock. Reaching around her, I push on the handle and open the door.

She hesitates at the threshold, and I fear she's about to change her mind. Taking matters into my own hands, I place one arm behind her back and sweep her legs out from beneath her. "Shit," she gasps as she leaves the floor.

Stepping into the room and shutting the door behind me, my heart hammers in my chest. But the second I look down at her, everything inside me settles.

I'm home.

"I'm not the one who needs carrying over the threshold tonight."

"Maybe not tonight, but one day." I've not considered what happens after I win her back. It wasn't my immediate concern, but now she's in my arms, I know without a doubt that one day in the near future I'm going to ask her to be mine officially.

Her chin drops as my words register in her head. "Trey, I—"

"Stop. Stop worrying about tomorrow. Next week. Next month. This is about us and tonight. Let me show you how things should be." Just in case she intends to argue, I drop her feet back to the ground and back her up against the wall.

"How. It. Should. Be."

My lips find hers, my tongue sweeping across her bottom one, encouraging her to open up for me. She hesitates for the briefest moment before she allows me entry, and my tongue immediately twists with hers. Her unique taste mixes with the lemonade she's been drinking all night, and my mouth waters.

Her hands grip the edges of my jacket so she can pull me tighter against her.

"Trey." Her breathy moan has my cock swelling and pressing against the zip of my trousers. "Give me your all."

Taking a step back, I pull her hands from me and her face drops. She just told me that she wants my all, so that's what she's going to fucking get. It took me years to be able to act on the dominant urges that have bubbled beneath my skin.

Sarah and I had a decent sex life in the beginning of our relationship, but we were just kids. I tried to push the limits a little as the years went on, but she was never really interested in the kinky stuff I wanted to experiment with. But now...now I've got Erica, who seems to be all for my kinky side, and if she wants me like our first night when I thought she was a stranger I'd never see again, then she'll damn well get it.

"Trey, what are you doing?" The panic in her voice makes me smile. She clearly doesn't understand how much she means to me if she's questioning whether this is going to happen or not. Nothing, and I mean nothing, could stop me from having her right now.

"Stand at the end of the bed, facing the pillows."

Her mouth drops open, defiance filling her face like she's about to tell me to go to hell. But then a small smile twitches at the corner of her mouth as she realises I'm just fulfilling her previous wish.

She drops her bag on the dresser as she passes and does exactly as she's told. My heart pounds in my chest as a million and one things I could do to her run through my head.

Slipping my jacket from my shoulders, I take my time in walking over and dropping it over the chair. Erica's heavy breathing is the only sound in the room. Knowing how much the anticipation is affecting her has me moving even slower.

I pop my cufflinks out, dropping them to the countertop. They bounce, and I delight in watching Erica flinch. She's so aware of her surroundings and my every action.

Tugging at my tie, I pull it through my collar and step up behind Erica. Sliding the silky fabric through my fingers, I lift my arms and place the slim teal fabric over her eyes.

She gasps but otherwise doesn't move as I secure it in place.

"This way, the sensation of every touch I give you will be increased." My lips gently brush over the smooth curve of her neck, and she shudders, her skin covered in goosebumps. She moans as I continue kissing down over her shoulder blade. The temptation to forget everything and just sink deep inside her is strong, but I'm stronger. It'll be worth it in the end.

"No," she complains when I step back once again, leaving her trembling.

"I'm not ready for you yet." It's a bare-faced lie, and she probably knows it. "I'll be back, don't move."

I imagine she thinks I'm joking, so I picture the look of horror on her face when the sound of the door opening and then slamming behind me sounds out around her.

Deciding to take the stairs, I jog down to the bar and place my order.

CHAPTER NINE

IN LESS THAN TEN MINUTES, I'm back and slipping Erica's key into the lock. Much to my delight, she's exactly where I left her.

"Good girl."

She growls in response. Perfect, she's gagging for it, just the way I like her.

Placing the tray in my hand down on the side, I make quick work of unbuttoning my shirt, pulling it from my arms and dropping it to the floor before toeing off my shoes and removing my socks. I leave my trousers in place, for now.

Grabbing the strawberry at the top of the giant pile I was given, I run it across Erica's full bottom lip. She gasps but is quick to follow instructions when I tell her to open up.

"Bite." She does, and the juice from the strawberry

runs down her chin. Stepping forward, I lick it up before continuing along the line of her jaw.

"Trey, please," she moans.

"What is it you need, sweetheart?"

"You."

"Hmmm." Reaching back, I grab another strawberry. "Open." She follows orders again, but this time I let the juice run down onto her chest before I clean her up.

Her dress was hardly containing her swollen tits earlier, but now they're fighting to be released.

"As much as I love this dress, I think it needs to go."

Kissing over her shoulder, I start the complicated task of undoing the lacing at her back.

"Fuck," I grunt when I allow the fabric to drop to her feet and find I've unwrapped a really fucking impressive present.

Her corset and thong are the exact shade of the dress and something dreams are made of.

"Your sister plan what you were wearing beneath this dress?"

She shakes her head.

"So you were expecting to spend the night with someone who'd appreciate it?" The thought of her spending tonight with someone who's not me has anger and jealousy swirling around uncomfortably in my stomach.

"No. I just wanted something nice. I didn't...I wouldn't..."

"Good answer."

Dropping down to my haunches, I tap her ankle and she lifts her foot, allowing me to move the dress. I do the same with the other side and push the fabric away. Placing her foot back to the floor, my fingertips slowly trail up the side of her leg as I stand. Her arse wiggles in my face as she tries to relieve the pressure building between her legs.

"No," I bark, sinking my teeth into the plump skin.

"Shit," she gasps in shock before bringing her hand around to rub the sting.

"Don't even think about giving yourself pleasure. That's for me and me only."

My fingers continue their journey up, dancing over the intricate patterns of her lace corset. If it wasn't so beautiful, I might rip it from her body, but it'd be a shame to waste something I could stare at her in every fucking day.

"You need more of these." Walking around so I can get a good look at the front of her, I understand why her breasts looked like they were about to pop out of her dress.

"Fuck me." A smug little smile appears on her red painted lips.

"Good, right?" Lifting her hand, she trails one of

her perfectly manicured fingertips along the fullness of her breasts. I allow her to continue for a few seconds just because the sight's too good to miss, but soon enough I'm batting her hand away.

"Enough," I bark, standing between her and the bed, forcing her to take a step back. Dropping my head, I lick across the edge of the corset and down into her cleavage. If it's possible I swear they swell even more.

"Jesus, Trey. I need...I need more. I need everything."

Lifting my hands, I unhook the first clasp on her corset. I'm just as desperate as she is to get her out of it and get my hands on what lies beneath.

"Yess," she hisses as the restrictive fabric starts to loosen around her body.

The second it's undone, I throw the fabric to the floor, take both her breasts in my palms and lift them to my lips. I suck one peaked nipple deep into my mouth making Erica moan and writhe under my touch.

They're more sensitve than I remember. I lick, suck and bite across both of them until she's almost at the point of no return. My name is a plea on her lips, but as much as I'd love to watch her come undone from this alone, there's no way in hell I'm letting her come until my cock's buried as deep inside her tight little pussy as physically possible.

"Fucking hell, Trey," she whines, reaching for me.

"You're forgetting who's in charge here, sweetheart."

Resting back on my palms, I take my time in running my eyes from the top of her head, over the silk fabric of my tie around her eyes, over her full, needy breasts and the soft curve of her waist before taking in her hips and mound that are still covered in copper lace.

"Take them off. I want to see all of you."

Tucking her thumbs into the fabric, she does exactly as she's told. Bending over, she puts on a show of pushing the scrap of fabric down and wiggling her hips to keep it moving.

Unable to hold back any longer, I reach out, wrap my hands around her tiny waist and lift her onto my lap.

I bring her close so her center rubs over my steel length and her breasts press against my chest. My fingers find their way into her intricate hairdo and force her lips to mine. Her mouth opens for me immediately, and she moans the second my tongue starts dancing with hers.

My fingers dig into the flesh at her hips as she tries to grind on me to find her release.

"Trey, please," she begs, "I'm gonna explode."

"Too fucking right you are. Lift up." She does as she's told and I push her upwards and lie back so the only thing I can see is her glistening pussy right above my face.

Pulling on her hips, I bring her down to meet my tongue. Her body shudders in my hands as I circle her clit again and again, driving her crazy. Sparks shoot through my body as her fingers twist in my hair and pull harshly in her attempt to get me closer, to get more of what she needs.

I chuckle against her and she moans in pleasure as the vibrations push her that little bit closer.

Lifting my head, I give her want she wants and suck her clit into my mouth. She cries my name and my chest swells. There have been times over the past two weeks that I really didn't think I'd be here again. I know we've still got a lot to work through, but surely this is a sign that she's going to forgive me and see where this thing between us goes.

Her body starts to tense above me, and I know she's nearing the end. Lifting her, I manage to maneuver us both so she's on her back and I'm standing at the edge of the bed, staring down at her as she squirms, her chest heaving and her tits rising and falling.

"If you don't let me come soon, you might not leave this room alive," she warns.

"Is that right?"

"Yeah. I really—" Her words are cut off as my hands go to my waistband seconds before my trousers and boxers drop to the floor. I kick them from my feet and crawl between her legs.

"You were saying?" Taking my length in my hand, I rub it though her juices, coating myself ready to slide into her.

"That I...That I need...*that*." She nods down to where I'm holding myself and bucks her hips to offer her entrance.

Lining myself up, I reach out my spare hand and entwine my fingers with hers, lifting her arms above her head.

"Ready?" A smirk pulls at my lips.

"Like you wouldn't fucking believe."

She barely gets the last word out because I thrust forward, ensuring that I fill her to the hilt in one smooth motion.

"Yes, Trey. Yes," she cries out, her hips shifting a little as she tries to adjust to my sudden invasion.

When I don't move again, she soon stops. "What? What's wrong?"

"Nothing." Letting go of her hand, I reach up to the tie around her head and slip it off. Her eyelids flutter as the light hits her, but her eyes soon find mine. "I need to see you. I want to watch your eyes as you fall apart."

"Please." Her hips grind, and I'm powerless to resist picking up the pace.

With her hands back in mine and my other on her hip to keep her in place, I thrust my hips forward again and again. Her tight walls ripple around me, and I soon find myself gritting my teeth in order to hold off my imminent release. All that teasing might have brought her right to the edge, but I was right along for the ride as well.

"Fuck, Trey. Fuck," she cries, her eyes not leaving mine for even a second.

"Come, Erica. Come all over my fucking cock," I grunt, holding back until she's found her own release.

On demand, her screams fill the room before her body locks up tight and she twitches and convulses beneath me. She loses her fight, and eventually the pleasure becomes too much, her eyes fluttering closed. I watch her ride out every second, committing the sight to memory before I allow my own release to consume me. I roar my long-awaited orgasm into the room as I fill her with everything I have.

I WAKE up a couple of times in the night and pull Erica closer to me. Everything seems right when her body's pressed up against mine, but just when I think everything's beginning to sort itself out, she throws me for a loop once again.

Coming to, I reach out to find her but her side of the bed is empty and cold. Pulling myself up so I'm sitting, I glance around the room. Seeing her dress still pooled on the floor where I left it, I relax, knowing that she can't have gone very far. Then I hear her.

She's in the bathroom, throwing up. Rushing from the bed, I crack the door open and peer in. The sight of her kneeling in front of the toilet with her head in the bowl damn near has me on my knees. I know it's morning sickness and that she's not really ill, but still, I hate it.

Rushing in, I place my hand on her back to do anything I can to help her, but she flinches at my touch.

"Don't."

The harshness in her voice has me standing and backing away.

"What's wrong?"

"Can you just leave, please." The sadness in her voice breaks my heart.

"Okay, I'll wait outside."

"No. I meant leave the hotel."

"But—"

She looks up at me with tears pooled in her eyes, and my words vanish.

"Last night was a mistake. It shouldn't have happened. I don't care what you say, I can't trust you.

One night of hot sex certainly won't change that. So please, just leave."

She heaves again, and I hesitate, but her hard, angry eyes hold mine, and I'm powerless.

"This isn't over, Erica. Not by a long shot."

CHAPTER TEN

IT'S BEEN two weeks since I walked out of that hotel and away from her. Two weeks since I heard her voice, since I touched her soft skin, since I looked into her vulnerable eyes and tried to prove to her that she can trust me.

Two weeks of pure hell.

I know she's okay, because Lauren gives me little updates every day, but I have no more information other than that she's alive. Every time I ask about Erica's pregnancy, Lauren's face gets all soft and sympathetic, and she just repeats that everything's fine. Fire burns through my veins every time I hear that damn word. 'Okay' could be a huge variety of things.

Every day after work, I knock on her door. Almost every day it goes unanswered, unless I'm late and Joe's already home. He neither confirms nor denies that she's inside, and every time he repeats that sentence, my fists clench at my sides. I have no desire to physically force my way in, but I'm bordering on desperate.

I find myself working more and more, or begging Sarah to spend more time with my girls. I need a distraction from the fact that Erica could be downstairs, pregnant with my baby.

One night when my desperation gets the better of me, I drive to Sam's house. I know they're away on honeymoon, and I wonder if Erica's staying there, but, just like her flat downstairs, no one answers the door.

I'm starting to give up hope that she'll ever allow me to see her again, let alone touch her, when a knock on my front door has my heart leaping into my chest. No one ever comes here—hell, most people from my life have no clue where I live since moving out of my old family home.

Putting my knife and fork down, I head over to the door and pull it open. I knew something was wrong the second the knock came, but the look on Joe's face as he stands on the other side is enough to have my stomach twisting in dread.

"What's wrong? Where's Erica? Is she okay?"

Refusing to meet my eyes, Joe asks if he can come in.

I rush to stand aside and, with his shoulders

slumped in defeat, he walks in and falls down onto my sofa.

"Joe, you're scaring the shit out of me. What's happened?"

"I shouldn't be here," he mumbles, his elbows on his knees and his head hanging low. "She'll kill me."

"Joe," I bark, fed up of his cryptic statements.

"Her mum's died."

"Shit. But she's okay?"

"I don't fucking know. I don't know what to do. She's locked herself in her room. She won't come out, she won't talk to me. I'm so fucking worried about her."

Looking up, the worry lines on his face are even more prominent, and the circles under his eyes seem darker.

"She's not eating, drinking...I don't know what the fuck she's thinking but—"

I don't need to hear any more. Pulling the front door open so wide it crashes back against the dresser behind, I run down the stairs as fast as my legs will carry me.

"Trey, what are you...*fuck*," Joe calls out behind me before he follows.

Our footsteps thunder down the stairs as we head towards their flat.

"Open the fucking door, or I'll break it down," I

shout as Joe rounds the corner a few seconds behind me.

He's as quick as he can be, sliding the key in the lock, but even that's too fucking slow.

"Get out of the fucking way." I shoulder barge him away from the door.

Pushing the key into the lock with a little more precision, I fling the door open in seconds and race towards her bedroom door.

"Erica?" I call. I wait for a beat just in case she responds, although from what Joe's just said I'm not expecting her to.

"She stopped talking to me a few days ago."

Fucking hell, Erica. What are you playing at?

"Erica, open the door or I'm going to break it down. I'm not letting you do this."

Silence greets us but, after a second, I hear the most blissful sound. Even though it's rough and full of emotion, it still makes my heart beat that little bit faster.

"Go away."

"Not going to happen, sweetheart. We're worried about you. Please let us in so we can look after you."

"I don't need you. I don't fucking need anyone."

"I know, I know." Agreeing with her pains me but she's right, she doesn't need anyone. She's strong and stubbornly independent, only, she's falling apart right now and can't do this alone. "We know, but we want to help.

"You've already done enough." A sob sounds out through the gap under the door, and my patience snaps.

I take two huge steps back before charging forward. My shoulder slams into the door, the wood splinters, and it swings open on twisted hinges.

"Fuck," I cry when I find Erica curled up in the center of her bed, sobbing into her pillow.

Racing towards her, I scoop her up into my arms and carry her from the room, much to Joe's horror.

"What the hell are you doing?" he fumes.

"What I should have been doing this whole time. Taking care of my woman."

He opens his mouth to argue but soon closes it again when he gets a look at the serious expression on my face.

"Shout if you need anything," he calls as I carry her out of their flat.

I know she's aware of what's going on. How could she not be, seeing as I've just lifted her from her own bed, but she doesn't move or make a noise aside from her subsiding sobs as I make my way back up to my flat.

Walking through the still wide open door, I come to a stop at the sofa and gently lower her.

"Don't move," I warn before heading to my bedroom to find her a blanket.

She's exactly where I left her when I reappear and wrap the soft fabric around her.

Dropping down to my haunches in front of her, I take her cold hands in mine. "What do you need, Erica? Tell me how to make this better and I'll do it. Please."

It takes a couple of seconds, but eventually her head lifts and her eyes find me. My breath catches and my heart aches looking back at her, so broken and tormented.

"Fuck, Erica." Releasing one hand, I reach out and take her face in my palm. The moment she leans into my touch, I know she's accepting my help. She doesn't need to say the words; I've always been able to know exactly what she needs without saying anything out loud.

"Don't move."

Standing, I stare down at her for a few seconds to make sure she doesn't need me to stay before heading into the kitchen. Thankfully, this flat is open plan, so as I get to work preparing her some food, I'm able to keep an eye on her. She has a tendency to run when things get hard, so I don't want to give her the opportunity to slip away from me now I've got her here.

My culinary skills aren't that great. Most of my life,

I've had someone else to cook for me. My mum is incredible in the kitchen, and I moved out of my parents' house into mine and Sarah's first place—she was at home taking charge of what we'd be eating, so I never really had a chance to hone my limited skills. Living by myself the past few months has been a bit of a challenge. Thank fuck I live in London and can have just about everything I could desire delivered.

Pulling a tub of chicken soup from the fridge that I picked up from a deli down the street a few days ago, I pull the top off and pour the contents into a saucepan. I grab the packet of part-baked bread I have in the cupboard and pop it into the oven.

While I wait for everything to heat up, I make her a coffee and take it over.

"Here, this might help."

"I...I can't drink coffee."

"It's decaf." Turning, her tired eyes find mine and they narrow in question. "I bought it hoping you'd come around one day."

A small smile twitches at her lips before she reaches out and lifts the steaming mug to her lips. She takes a hesitant sip before her eyelids flutter in pleasure.

"I did some research to find out what brand was the best. Just because you can't have the caffeine, it doesn't mean it should taste like shit."

"Thank you," she whispers, the sadness of her voice almost ripping my heart in two.

"I'm sorry to hear about your mum. I can't imagine how you must be feeling."

"Empty."

I open my mouth to say something, but I soon realise I've no idea what to say to that. I'm lucky, I've still got both my parents.

"Please let me help. I'll do anything to make this easier on you."

She looks at me over the top of her mug. I can tell she's fighting what's on the tip of her tongue, but after a couple of seconds she says it anyway. "You already are."

Warmth spreads through my body, knowing that I'm a comfort to her right now, maybe even proving myself, who knows.

The timer dings on the oven, breaking our moment.

"I'll be right back." She grants me a small smile before I get up, confirming to me that I'm helping.

I make quick work of getting it dished up before returning with it laid out on a tray. "Chicken soup and warm bread," I say when she looks over inquisitively. "When was the last time you ate?"

"I had a packet of rich tea biscuits in my room."

"Well, that's okay then," I say lightly.

A humourless noise passes her lips as she sits up straighter so I can place the tray on her lap.

I allow her time to eat, although she only has a few spoonfuls of soup and a couple of chunks of bread before she places it onto the coffee table.

"I can only have little bits at a time or I'll throw up." Turning herself so she's sitting in the corner of the sofa, she looks up at me through her lashes.

"Talk to me, please, Erica."

She blows out a long breath, making me think she's going to ignore my demand, but eventually she looks away and starts explaining.

"I got the phone call from the care home in the middle of the night. She's been in that place for so long that I started to think she'd just be there forever and that my Sundays would always be taken up visiting her. It really threw me for a loop. My first instinct was to pick up the phone to call my sister, but there was a reason I was the first person they told."

"She's on honeymoon," I mutter, putting two and two together.

"Yeah. I had no idea what to do for the best. I didn't want to ruin their time away. Our parents have already managed to ruin most of our lives—this was one time in her life that I wanted Sam to just forget about everything and enjoy herself."

"Have you told her?"

"I rang a couple of days ago. I wanted to have organised everything before I told her so she wouldn't have any reason to come back early."

"You've organised everything?"

"Why is that such a surprise? I'm more than capable." Her face hardens and I panic, thinking that she's about to start shutting down on me.

"I know that, sweetheart. I was more thinking that you didn't have to deal with everything alone."

"No one else needs to be dragged into my bullshit. Anyway, I didn't have a lot to do. It's not like I have any relatives to notify or invite to the funeral, and there's not any hidden millions for Sam and I to argue over."

"When is the funeral?"

"Tomorrow."

"What time? I'll go with you."

"I'm not going." Clearly not wanting to argue about it, she turns away from me.

"Erica. I really think—"

"No. You don't get to think anything. You've no idea about my childhood and my mother. There's no way you could understand how I feel now she's gone. You had the perfect upbringing with doting parents; it's a million miles away from how I lived."

"You're right. I'll never understand, but I want to

support you, and I think no matter what's happened in the past, she's still your mother, and one day you'll regret not going. You'll only get one chance at tomorrow—whether that's to say goodbye or just to start a new chapter in your life, I think it's important."

She lets out a huge sigh. "I'll think about it."

"You can just admit that I'm right, you know?"

"No chance." Her lips curl up, and I find just a little bit of the Erica I know and love hiding behind all the betrayal and heartache.

Silence stretches out between us as I think about the fact that I caused most of said heartache.

"Erica?" I ask, feeling the sudden need to confess how I really feel.

When she doesn't respond, I look over, finding her fast asleep.

I get up as quietly as I can and tidy up what's left from dinner before sliding my hands under her and carrying her down to my bedroom. She's dressed in a pair of leggings and an oversized t-shirt. As much as I might want to strip her down so I can feel her skin against mine, I know it's not what she'll want. So I just pull the covers back tand place her down gently.

"Thank you," falls from her lips as she curls up, her breathing instantly slowing as she falls back to sleep.

I might want to crawl in next to her, but I know it's too early for me to be able to fall asleep.

Grabbing my laptop, I fall into the chair at the other side of the room and continue scrolling through the same website I was searching through before leaving for work this morning, looking for the perfect family house.

CHAPTER ELEVEN

I WAKE up much like I did the morning in the hotel after Sam's wedding: alone in a cold bed with the sound of her throwing up filtering through from the en suite.

Hoping that might be where the similarities end, I quickly make my way to her. I don't say anything as I enter, assuming that the squeaky door is enough to announce my entrance.

Dropping down beside her, I take her hair in one hand and rub her back with the other. She tenses for a second, but, unlike last time, she relaxes before heaving once again.

I sit silently beside her, hoping that I might be helping but feeling completely useless. I wish I could take it all away from her.

"I CAN'T WAIT for this stage to be over," she says, dropping my toothbrush back into the glass and finding my horrified eyes in the mirror. "What? What's that look for?" Shaking my head, I push aside the fact that she stole my toothbrush and focus on what's really important.

"Are you..." I hesitate, because I'm sure no pregnant woman wants to be asked the question I need the answer to. "Are you keeping it?"

"Are you fucking kidding me?" Erica runs from the room faster than I've ever seen her move before. "How can you even ask me that?"

Racing after her, I wrap my fingers around her wrist. She stops but keeps her back to me. "Because I don't know, Erica. I've no idea how you feel about this."

"Does it matter? You told me that you didn't want any more kids."

"No, I told you that I didn't *think* I did. But that was before any of this." Spinning her around, I place my hands on her cheeks so she's got no choice but to look into my eyes. "Finding out you were pregnant was the shock of my life, but," I continue when she looks like she's about to interrupt, "I want it all with you, Erica. I want the house, the babies, the forever. And do you know why?" She shakes her head as much as I'll allow with my hands cupping her face. "Because I love you, Erica Wilde. I love you so fucking much that it scares the shit out of me." The tears that were filling her eyes spill over and hit my thumbs.

Pulling her trembling body to mine, I wrap my arms around her as she sobs. Dropping my nose to her hair, I breathe her in and immediately relax. We stand there long after her sobs have passed, just holding each other.

Eventually, I take a few steps backwards and drop us both down to the edge of the bed.

Pulling her arms from my shoulders, I force her back a little so I can look into her eyes. I hate to end our embrace, but it's important.

"What time is the funeral?"

"Ten-thirty," she whispers. Glancing over the top of her head, I notice the time on the alarm clock next to my bed.

"Shit, we'd better get moving."

"Do I have to?"

"If you really don't want to, I'll respect that, but I really think—"

Placing her fingers over my lips, she stares into my eyes. "No, you're right. I'd regret it."

"We'd better get moving then." She lifts an eyebrow in question.

"Yeah, *we*. I'm not letting you do this alone."

I expect her to argue, but instead all she does is to drop her head back to my shoulder.

"As much as I'd love to spend the rest of the day with you in my arms, we've got something we need to do first."

"I don't want to."

"I know, sweetheart. I know."

Threading my fingers into her hair, I pull her face from my shoulder so I can find her lips. Her kiss is hesitant and gentle, and as much as my body urges me to push her into something more passionate, I know it's what she needs right now.

Nonetheless, my cock swells inside my boxers, and, when I lift her from my lap and place her back down on the bed, it's making a nice tent.

"Good morning, Mr. Bennett." Her eyes run down my naked chest until she finds my excitement. Her teeth sink into her bottom lip and her eyes darken.

"Stop getting ideas, we don't have time."

"We could do it instead."

"Nice try."

Turning my back to her, I pull my wardrobe open and find my black suit. I grab a clean pair of boxers before dropping the pair I'm wearing to the sounds of Erica's frustrated groan.

She says nothing, but when I glance back at her, I know she's scheming up her revenge.

"Okay, let's go downstairs so you can get ready," I say once I've made two coffees—one decaf—and put them into travel mugs ready for the journey.

"Morning," Joe says, racing towards the front door when Erica unlocks it.

"What are you doing here?"

"I've got the day off to accompany you. Not that it looks like you need it now."

Stepping away from me, she walks up to Joe and throws her arms around him. "I'm so sorry."

"It's okay, sweets."

"Did you still get to go out last night?"

"Yeah, I knew you were in safe hands."

"I'll be as quick as I can." After releasing him, Erica races down to her bedroom. I'm desperate to follow, but with Joe's eyes boring into me like he wants to talk, I stay put.

"Go anywhere nice last night?" I didn't pay any attention at the time, my concern solely on Erica, but the memory of him standing at my door dressed in a white shirt with braces and thick-rimmed glasses fills my mind. It's not a look I've seen on him before.

"Oh...uh...just meeting a friend?"

I quirk my eyebrow at him, not believing a word of it, but he quickly changes the subject. "So, how's she doing?"

"Well, I've convinced her to go today, so I take that as a win."

"Has she told you about her childhood? Her parents?"

"Snippets but I think there's probably a lot more to it."

Nodding, he stares off into the distance. "Did you know them?"

"Who?"

"Her parents."

"Oh, no. We've only known each other for about five years. I can just sympathise, having my own fucked up parents." He shakes his head. "But that's a story for another day. It's Erica we need to be focusing on right now."

I couldn't agree more, but I'm now even more intrigued than ever about Joe. He seems to have mastered the skill of keeping everyone around him at arm's length, and it frustrates the hell out of me.

When Erica reappears, all my thoughts about Joe vanish. She looks incredible in her simple black dress that hugs her slightly more curvaceous body. But it's the look on her face that captivates me. Her pain and grief shine in her eyes, but her face is twisted, showing her lack of confidence as she stands there under our stares. It's unnerving to see it, because she's always been so confident and sure of herself.

Pushing myself from the sofa, I walk up to her and take her hands in mine.

"What's wrong?"

"My dress doesn't fit," she whispers sadly.

"Weird, because it looks fucking awesome to me."

"I feel huge already."

"You look beautiful." Standing back, I allow my eyes to drop, and I take my time running them over every one of her curves. I need her to understand just how much she captivates me. Yes, her curves are sexy, but hell, she could hide them under a black bag and I'd still be drawn to her. "If we didn't have to go out right now, I'd show you just how good you look. But for now, just know how much you affect me." Stepping back towards her, I place her hand against my thick length. "I just want you, Erica. Baby bump, stretch marks and all. I promise you that nothing will put me off."

Hope shines in her eyes, but as soon as she blinks it's gone. She doesn't want to believe it, just like she doesn't want to believe how I feel about her or how she really feels about me. It's not lost on me that I told her I loved her earlier and she didn't say it back. But I feel it. I feel it every time she looks at me, with every touch of our bodies. She just believes that living in denial will make it all easier. Sadly for her, I'm not going to allow that.

I wasn't really sure what I was expecting from

today, but it certainly wasn't the very small welcoming party we had waiting for us at the local crematorium. I recognise every single person standing by the entrance as I drive towards the car park with Erica to my left and Joe practically filling the entire back seat of my car. The second we're spotted, Sam starts running and Erica begins fumbling with the seat belt. The moment I park, I help her out and press the button allowing her to jump from the car and into her sister's arms.

They stand and cry together as Joe and I get out and come to stand beside them. Cliff, Sam's new husband, comes over to join us, along with Lauren and Ben. Ben shakes my hand, his over-the-top protectiveness on full display in his eyes.

"How's she doing?" he whispers when he tugs me towards him.

"Surviving. Just be glad she's here."

"She wasn't going to?"

I shake my head, but I swallow down the words I was going to say when Erica snuggles into my side, her cheeks damp with tears and eyes rimmed red.

"Thank you for coming," she says to Lauren and Ben.

"Shut up. As if we'd be anywhere else."

"I really appreciate it."

"You being nice to him?" Lauren asks, flicking her eyes up at me.

"As nice as he deserves."

"Good luck, Trey. This one knows how to hold a grudge."

"I do not," Erica sulks.

"Are you kidding? You didn't talk to me for about a week not long after we met because you didn't get your own way."

"He's totally lying. It was like thirty minutes," she says, looking up at me with a smile on her face.

Silence falls over our small group as people start to leave the crematorium from the previous funeral.

"You ready for this, kid?" Sam asks, once again wrapping her arm around Erica's shoulders.

"So ready." It's an odd thing to say. I can't imagine it would be my reaction to a parent's funeral, but then I've had a very different upbringing to them both, so I keep my mouth shut and follow their lead.

"I can't believe you did all of this yourself, you nutcase."

"It was time I took control for once and allowed you to enjoy yourself."

"I love you, kid. You know that, right?" Sam ruffles Erica's hair, much to her disgust.

The seven of us walk in and take seats at the front. A few others eventually join us, but when Erica points out that they're carers from the home, my heart aches for everything she must have been through, not having anyone but her sister to support her. The more and more I learn about her, the more I understand why she shields her heart quite so fiercely.

The ceremony is...quick. Erica said that she didn't think her mum deserved too much fuss and, from the length of the service and the lack of anyone standing up to say any words, it's clear that she really meant it. It's so sad that a mother can have both her children at her funeral and neither are willing to stand up and say anything about who she was. It makes me want to go and find my girls and hold them that little bit tighter so they know that, although I may no longer be at home with them, I've by no means stopped caring. I make a note to text them both when I get a moment.

"What's next?"

"I just booked a table for the four of us. Seemed pointless planning an actual wake." I can't really argue with that, so after we've said goodbye to the others, I follow Sam and Cliff to the restaurant Erica chose.

"Were you expecting that kind of turn out?" I ask as we drive away from the crematorium.

"Less, actually. I had no idea Lauren and Ben we're coming or the carers. I just thought it would be Sam and Cliff." She sighs and looks out the window.

"Our child will never experience anything you did, and you're going to be an incredible mum." She sniffs, and I know my words are getting to her. "If your own experiences have taught you anything, it's how not to do it."

"Something good's got to come from it," she agrees, a humourless laugh falling from her.

THE RESTAURANT'S a quaint little place on the outskirts of the city.

"Why here?"

"I just wanted to get away for a bit. Leave it all behind."

"Me?"

"Huh?"

"You wanted to leave me behind?"

Her eyes soften as she blows out a breath. "No, I—"

"It's okay. This isn't the time for this conversation. Let's go and have an incredible meal, and then I've got a surprise for you."

"What is it?"

"It's a surprise, so it should be obvious that I can't tell you."

"It better be bloody good," she mutters as she gets out and joins Sam and Cliff.

"A word?" Sam says, her small hand holding my forearm to stop me and to allow Erica and Cliff to walk off ahead.

"She's been hurt time and time again, but this time it was different. This time it really hurt, and that's because it's real. I see the connection between you—it's why I didn't send you on your way on our wedding day. I can see how much you love her, more than anyone in her past. She's going to try to ruin this whichever way she can because she thinks being heart-broken and alone is what she deserves for some fucked up reason I'm yet to fully understand. If you want her, you're going to need to fight like hell. She might forgive you this time, but she'll find another reason to push you away. Maybe not tomorrow, or next week or month, but she will, and you're going to have to cling on for dear life as she tries to self-destruct. Are you ready for that? And more importantly, can you continue holding on? Because if the answer is no, you need to let go now before you get in too deep."

"I'm not going anywhere, Sam. You can trust me."

"I know that, but I'm not the important one."

"I've got her...I've got them."

"That's what I thought."

"What's going on?" Erica asks when we get to where she's holding the door open, waiting for us to join them.

"Sam was just giving me her big sister speech."

"Please tell me you weren't," she begs Sam.

"What?" she asks innocently. "I don't care how old or ugly he is, I need to look out for my kid sister."

"I don't need looking out for."

"No, but I want to, and you're stuck with me, so suck it up, sista."

They both laugh as they walk through the entrance to the restaurant arm-in-arm. It's nowhere near what anyone would expect on the day they said goodbye to their mother, but after everything they've been through, it's good to see the smiles on their faces. It'll take a hell of a lot more than today to break them.

CHAPTER TWELVE

"ARE you going to tell me what it is yet?" Erica asks once she's woken up from her nap. We'd only been in the car a few minutes before her head dropped back and she was gone.

The meal was probably the longest of my life as Erica picked at her bland food in an attempt to not spend the entire time we were there in the toilets. It worked because, as far as I'm aware, she's not thrown up since first thing this morning.

"Mornin'," I say with a chuckle.

"Laugh away, but this whole growing a person thing is exhausting. I can only imagine what it'll be like when I'm the size of a whale."

"You won't be the size of a whale."

"You wanna bet? I saw pictures of Mum when she

was pregnant with both me and Sam, and she was colossal."

"Doesn't mean you will be. Anyway, it doesn't matter if you are, you'll still be gorgeous."

"Hmm...we'll see."

"Does that mean you're keeping me around long enough to see you that pregnant?"

"This is your baby too, Trey. Regardless of what happens between the two of us, I'd never take him from you."

"Him?" I ask, trying to push aside the emotion her words drag up my throat.

"Yeah, I just feel like it might be a boy."

A wide smile finds its way onto my lips. I can't deny that I wouldn't love to have a son, especially already knowing what dealing with teenage daughters is like.

"Would you be willing to meet my girls?"

Her head snaps around to me, the shock of my question clear on her face. I know it might be a bit much, but I fully intend on having Erica in my life for a long time to come, so it's important that she meets my girls sooner rather than later. Ella already knows about Erica and is rightly concerned after what she's overheard her mother talking about. I want them to meet her so they can fall in love with her, just like I have.

"One day," she agrees, and that's good enough for me. She's got a lot to process right now; I don't want to put more on her. "Are we visiting someone?" she asks when she looks back out the window and realises that we're driving down a residential street filled with well-maintained terraced Victorian houses.

"No, I want to show you something."

"Here?"

"Here. Come on."

A frown creases her brow as she accepts my hand and allows me to pull her from the seat to join me on the pavement.

"These houses are stunning. I bet they're seriously expensive."

"They're not cheap, that's for sure."

I bring her to a stop between two cars just up ahead and pull her across the road once it's clear.

"This is the one."

"Ooookay."

She follows me up to the front door and waits to discover what's about to happen when I knock.

It only takes a second or two for the door to open, and a young woman dressed in a suit greets us.

"Mr. Bennett, it's good to see you. And this must be Miss Wilde?"

"Yeah, hi."

"Hello, I'm Leanne. Come on in."

Leanne's aware that this is a surprise, which is why she doesn't explain who she is. "I'll leave you guys to it. If you need me, I'll be outside. Please take your time."

Erica's silent as Leanne walks out the front door, leaving us in the house alone.

"Trey, what the hell is going on?"

"Come on, let's look around."

"Why?" It's like she nails her feet to the floor, because when I move she point-blank refuses.

"Trey?"

"Humour me?"

Blowing out a frustrated breath, she agrees and follows me towards a room that turns out to be the kitchen. Surely she's figured out where this is going, but I want her to look around before we get into an argument about the future.

"Wow," she breathes, expressing my exact thoughts when I saw it online this morning. The kitchen is an extension from the back of the house. Its back wall consists of huge sliding doors which allow so much light in—combine that with the sky lights, and it's almost like being in an outside kitchen.

Each room gets better and better as we walk around, but it's not until we're in the smallest of the four bedrooms that I take Erica's hand and pull her into my body.

"So what do you think?"

"I think it's stunning, how could I not? It's for sale, isn't it?"

"It is. We're the first, and depending on what you're about to say, the only people to view it."

"Trey, this is crazy. There's no way I can afford to live somewhere like this. My flat is a serious stretch every month. I have no savings. I can't even dream—"

"Stop, please," I beg, cupping her chin with my fingers. "I'm not asking about your financial situation. I'm asking if you want to live here. Can you picture yourself in his house...in this room, nursing our baby?"

Stepping away from me, she pulls out the office chair that's neatly tucked under the desk in here and lets out a sigh, her hand protectively falling on her belly. She's probably totally unaware of the move, and it's one of the reasons I know she's going to be an incredible mum.

"This is crazy, Trey."

"I couldn't agree more. But—" I fall down at her feet. I take her free hand in mine and place my other hand next to hers on her belly. "I'm in love with you, Erica. You're mine, both you and the little peanut in here. If we're doing this, I refuse to do it in a little flat with a lift that works some of the time. I've always given my kids everything they could possibly need, and this little one is no different."

"But—"

"No more buts. We both know them all. Stop worrying about what might happen and focus on what you want. Drop those walls a little and start listening to your heart, not your head. How do you picture your future, Erica? Is it with me and our baby?"

Slowly, she starts nodding. "Of course I want to be with you and our baby. And this house is incredible—it's more than I could ever dream of. I'm just scared."

"I know you are. Trust me, I am too. The idea of having a newborn again scares the shit out of me, but I know we can do it...just like I know we can as a couple. We're meant to be, sweetheart. Take the chance with me, please?"

"I don't have time to really think about this, do I?"

"You can have as much time as you need, but you might have to picture a different house when you do it. This place will be snapped up by the end of the day, either by us or by someone. Trust me when I say there aren't many like this around."

"You've been looking for a house for us?"

"I've been looking for a place before I even moved out, but I hadn't been able to find the right one. When I discovered your pregnancy, my priorities changed from bachelor pad to family home."

"You're really serious about this, aren't you?"

"Yeah. If you want this house, it's yours, sweetheart."

"I don't want you to buy me a house."

"Okay, well, we can put yours on the market and you can put whatever you get into this place if it makes you feel better. I'll be truly ours then."

She chews on her bottom lip as she mulls over my suggestion. Just that one simple move has me hard as fuck and ready to christen every single room in this house.

"How much is this place even up for?"

"We'll discuss that once you decide. The price doesn't matter."

She narrows her eyes at me, clearly unhappy with the amount I'm willing to spend.

"And you have the money to buy this place, just like that?"

"We'll probably need a small mortgage. I'm not that rich."

"The fact that you're even searching for houses like this suggests you're pretty loaded." Her mouth drops to a frown, and she turns away from me.

"What's wrong?"

"You're here suggesting we buy this insane house, yet I don't know the most basic of things about you. I know most of it is probably not all that important, but I want to know it all."

"It does matter. I want to know it all too. But our relationship was never going to be conventional, so while others might learn all that stuff while they're dating, we can do it while we're here, together."

"*If* I were to agree to this. How long until we move in?"

I can't help the smile that twitches at my lips at the knowledge that she's already considering moving in. I know she's holding back, because the sensible side of her brain is telling her to protect herself, but her heart is all in.

"We can move in whenever you like. If you want to wait, maybe date for a little while, then we can."

My words seem to perk her back up. She jumps from the chair and walks from the room. She's halfway up the stairs to the converted loft room when I catch up with her.

"Wow, this room is gorgeous."

"When I found it online, I thought it might be a nice room for Ella and Sofia for when they come to stay, but now I'm seeing it, I'm not sure I'd want to give it up."

Erica's deep in thought as she wanders around the room and pokes her head into the walk-in wardrobe.

"If I agree to meet your daughters, can we keep this room?" I can see the trepidation in her eyes when she talks about them. I know she's having a hard time trying to accept me having a past before her, I understand that. But I think she's making it out to be worse in her head and that things will seem better once they've met and she realises they're not all that scary.

"You can have whatever you want."

"Hmmm."

The walk back down to the ground floor is in silence. I've no idea what she's really thinking, but my heart races as I glance into each room we pass, seeing her in them with our baby in her arms. I picture her in the kitchen at a high chair feeding, curled up on the sofa with a baby on her chest as they nap together. I can hear the laughter and joy of a family that used to make me feel so complete before everything started to derail.

I'm still lost in my thoughts as I follow Erica through the front door to find Leanne, the estate agent, on her phone at the front of the house.

"Oh," she says quickly stuffing it into her pocket. "What did you think? It's a beautiful house, right? It'll be snapped right up."

"We'll have it," Erica interrupts, shocking both Leanne and myself.

"We will?" I ask, sliding my arm around her waist and pulling her to me. She stares up at me, a slight frown between her brows. I run my eyes over every inch of her beautiful face while my heart races so fast I think it might just explode.

"Just make me one more promise?"

"Anything."

"Don't make me regret it."

"Never." Lowering my lips to her, I pepper kisses across them, but she soon gets greedy and opens for me. As I sweep my tongue past her lips, her taste explodes in my mouth, making my cock ache for her. Everything surrounding me vanishes, and it just becomes the two of us embarking on the rest of our lives together.

Leanne clears her throat, and I regretfully pull away.

Still staring down at Erica once I've put some space between us, I say "Yes, we'll have it. Full asking price. Let's get it moving."

"Sure thing, Mr Bennett, Miss Wilde. You've got a hell of a house here. I'll be in touch with details ASAP."

CHAPTER THIRTEEN

"IS it wrong that I don't want to leave?" Erica asks with a laugh.

Leanne left us to it ages ago, promising to confirm our offer as soon as she contacted the seller, leaving me to get in touch with my financial advisor to sort out the financial side.

"No, I think that's a really good sign. I'd move in right now if I could."

"Are you sure you don't think this is too fast?"

"I wasn't aware there were rules to this kind of thing. I'm just going by what I want and what I think is best for our new family." Placing my hands on her flat belly, I stare down at her in amazement. "You're growing our baby. How incredible is that?"

"Do you still think so, even though you've been through it twice before?"

"Is that something you're worried about? That this isn't my first time?"

"Yeah." She tries to cast her eyes away, but I capture her cheek and force them back to me. "I've no clue what I'm doing, and I'd kind of like it if you were equally as clueless."

She frowns when I laugh, but I can't help it. "Don't worry, I feel totally clueless. Having my girls feels like a lifetime ago. Plus, I wasn't really around much in the early days, so it will feel like it's the first time."

"Why weren't you around?"

"I worked too much," I say regretfully. "Sarah's dad had a small building firm. I'd worked there my entire life until I made the decision to leave her. That day, I waked away from my wife, my kids, my house, and my job. He told me I could stay, but I needed a fresh start. Still working there would keep me tied to the family more. I'd bump into Sarah regularly, and I didn't want to make it harder on any of us. I'd been there since he offered me an apprenticeship at sixteen. It was all I'd ever known, but it was the right thing to do. So when I heard about the job at Johnson & Sons, I knew I couldn't turn it down. A small family firm that was in need of rescuing was right up my street. You've no fucking idea how happy I am that I took the job."

"It's a pretty great place to work."

"Does that mean you'll come back?"

"I...uh..."

"Don't stop doing something you love because you want to punish me. You'd told me before how much you need it. I know Ben and Lauren are desperate to have you back."

"I'll speak to them about it."

"Is that a yes?"

Her lips twitch with excitement and her green eyes sparkle in a way I've missed so fucking much. "It's a maybe."

"Whatever you say." I chuckle. "Come on, I've got more planned for today."

"Where now?"

"Wait and see."

We drive for a few minutes before pulling up into a retail park. Erica sits nervously beside me as she stares at the huge baby shop in front of us.

"Are you okay? You look like you're about to puke."

"Uh...I think I might."

"Why?"

"Just looking at that place makes it all seem so real. I'm not sure I'm ready. I can barely look after myself."

"Bullshit," I snap, a little too harshly if her flinching is anything to go by. "Sorry. It's just that you've been looking after yourself pretty much your whole life, from what you've told me. This will be a walk in the park for you."

"I've never even held a baby," she whispers, her cheeks brightening with the confession.

"Neither had I before Ella came along." Slipping my hand into hers, I squeeze in support. "You'll be the best mum, Erica, I have no doubt. You're so caring and supportive. Our little one will be lucky to have you."

She sniffles and fights the tears pooling in her eyes, but there's a smile on her face. "Damn you. I'm pretty sure I've cried more in the last few weeks than I have in my life."

"I think that's pretty standard. It's the hormones."

"That should have clued me in on what was going on, really. I was an emotional mess."

"How did you find out?"

"It was Ben. He said something about me being emotional like a pregnant woman, and I freaked out. With everything I'd been experiencing, it made total sense."

"That was the day you went home sick." I think back to how she must have felt. "Why didn't you tell me that night?" I don't mean for it to come out as an accusation, but it does nonetheless.

"I was terrified, Trey. I'd done the bloody test in a Starbuck's toilet because I couldn't wait to get home to find out the truth. I had no idea what you'd think. If you'd think I'd done it on purpose or something. We barely knew—we barely *know* each other. Hell, I didn't know how to react."

"It's okay. I understand that you needed time to process it."

"I was going to tell you that night at the restaurant. I'd spent all day practicing my speech but then—" She lets out a sigh.

"I ruined it."

"Something like that," she says sadly. "You should have just told me about her at the beginning. I wouldn't have cared."

"I know. I just didn't expect...well, any of this. I didn't think I'd see you again after that night, and then when I did I just got swept away. You were everything I'd ever wanted, and I knew I was going to ruin it."

"Wasn't Sarah everything you ever wanted?" I open my mouth to respond, but she beats me to it. "I'm sorry, I'm just trying to understand."

"I thought she was, but we were so young. When she had the girls, our lives became about them. We never took the time to think about us, aside from a date night every few weeks where we mostly let out a deep breath, just glad to have a few hours of peace. We'd grown apart over the years, like I said before. We'd been travelling down different paths. I wanted more and she wanted to stay the same."

Her face twists in uncertainty.

"What is it? I'll tell you anything."

"Were you...when you were..." she blows out a breath and decides to just get to the point. "Was your sex life like ours is?"

"Wow. Erica Wilde, seductress extraordinaire, is shy about asking a sex question," I say with a laugh.

"Trey," she groans.

"No, sweetheart. It was nothing like us." That seems to settle whatever she was worried about. "You ready to do this?" I nod towards the shop.

"No, I'm really not."

"That's a shame, because we're going in."

She's still in the car when I get around to her side, pulling the door open, I reach into take her hand. "I promise it won't be as scary as you're making it out to be in your head. We're just going to look. Just think how cute that little room will be full of nursery furniture."

"I guess," she mutters, allowing me to pull her out.

She's silent as we walk through the sliding doors. I watch as she looks at the pushchairs directly in front of us before she glances around the shop.

The colour drains from her face before she pulls

her hand from mine. "I can't do this. It's too much. I don't even know where to start."

"We start with the maternity clothes. You're going to need some, right? Have you bought new bras yet?"

"New bras?" she asks, the movement of her chest starting to increase with her panic.

"Come on, we're just clothes shopping."

We do three laps of the maternity clothes. Erica selects a couple of items before she comes to stop in front of a display of newborn baby clothes.

I stand aside slightly as she reaches out and runs her fingertips across the front of the soft fabric. She glances down at her belly and then back to the babygrow, biting her bottom lip.

"Is he really going to be this small?" she asks when I come to stand beside her and pull her into my arms.

"He might even be smaller."

"Smaller! How is that even possible?"

"Why, did you want to push a bigger one out?"

Her lips press into a flat line as she considers my question. "Christ, what have I got myself into?"

"Come on, let's have a look at the nursery furniture."

"How are we meant to choose? It's all so cute."

"Do you want to find out the sex?"

"Um...I don't know. Do you?"

"I don't mind. It just might help with picking."

"But what if we have another?"

"Do you want more?"

"I've no idea. I'm not sure I'm going to know how to deal with this one. Let's see if I can do that before discussing the possibility."

"Okay, let's stick with neutral then, just in case."

"Jesus. I can't believe I'm doing this with a man I don't even live with."

"That can be fixed." *And soon, hopefully.* "What about this one? I like the oak."

"Yeah, me too."

For someone who I thought was going to refuse to walk any farther than the door, she didn't seem to want to leave after what was probably our fourth lap of the place. We left with a stack of new clothes for her, along with a couple of bras and a *What to expect when you're expecting* book in the hope it'll give her some confidence about what's to come and to prove that she's more than well-equipped to be a mother.

"You hungry?"

"Yeah, as long as the food's bland."

"Uh...McDonalds?"

"Perfect."

Erica orders a kids meal, explaining that she thinks a full meal would be too much, but then proceeds to polish off two McFlurry's like they're going out of fashion.

"What's so funny?"

"Nothing, sweetheart."

"You think I'm a pig, don't you?"

"Not at all. You can have anything that makes you feel better."

CHAPTER FOURTEEN

WE'RE HALFWAY home when the sound of my phone ringing fills the car. Glancing down at the screen, I see my ex-wife's name staring back at me.

I look over to Erica, who's also staring at it, wondering what to do.

"It's okay. You can get it. I'll be quiet."

"I'll be quick, I promise."

She nods, then turns to look out the window.

Hitting accept, I wait for her voice to fill my ears. It might be familiar, but it doesn't affect me in any way. It hasn't for a very long time.

"Trey, I need your help. Ella and I have had a...disagreement. She's refusing to come out of her room and demanding to see you."

"Uh...what do you want me to do?"

"Come and talk to her. Tell her that she's too young to be going out with boys."

"She's fourteen, Sarah. Isn't that what kids do?"

"Not my kid, and not with the boy she wants to go out with."

"But—"

"No buts. I need you to back me up on this one and trust that I'm right."

"You know that stopping her will only make her more determined to do it."

"I don't care. I'm not letting her spend time with that...tyrant."

Letting out a frustrated breath, I glance over at Erica, whose shoulders are pulled tight with tension. "Give me an hour, and I'll be there."

"An hour? This has already been going on long enough. Can't you be here any sooner? I need to go out."

"So just go out. She'll be fine sulking."

"Or sneaking out."

"Do you mind if we go over?" I whisper to Erica.

"Is that her?" Sarah snaps.

"Enough. Do you want my help or not?"

"Fine."

"Give me a minute, I'll call you back."

Sarah complains, but she hangs up nonetheless.

"I can drop you off if you don't want to come."

Erica is silent for a few seconds before she turns back to look at me, her face set with determination.

"No, if we're really doing this...us, then I'm coming with you." Her eyes narrow, and I can't help but feel like she's testing me somehow.

"It might not be pleasant. Sarah's not exactly your biggest fan."

"I'm sure I've dealt with worse."

The reminder of her past twists my stomach like it always does. I wish I could go back and erase it all for her.

"Okay then. Let's do this." My voice comes out sounding much more confident than I feel. Erica is wrong if she thinks I want to hide her. I'm more than happy for anyone to see us together. I'm more concerned about her and my daughters than I am about Sarah's opinion of our new relationship.

Redialing her number from my steering wheel, she picks up on the first ring. "We'll be there in twenty."

"We?"

"We." Hanging up, I blow out a calming breath, trying to imagine what kind of mother-daughter war I'm about to walk into. It's not the first. Ella and Sarah clash on the best of days, and I'm sure it won't be the last.

"You sure you want to do this now? Today's already been pretty stressful."

"Yes, I'm sure."

"Okay, well...let's do this then."

Climbing from the car, Erica joins me and, hand in hand, we walk towards my old front door and I ring the bell. The time has long past that I felt able to just walk in. My name might still be on the deeds for this place, but it's by no means my home anymore. Home is where the heart is, and that's wherever Erica is.

It's only a few seconds before the sounds of footsteps running down the stairs rings out and the door's pulled open.

Sarah doesn't even bother looking at me. Her eyes zero straight in on Erica.

"Christ, Trey, she looks even younger than I remember."

I go to say something, but Erica beats me to it. My chest swells with pride that she's confident enough in us to stand up to my ex-wife.

"Hi, I'm Erica, but I'm sure you remember that from when you gatecrashed our date. My age isn't really any business of yours, and neither is what your *ex*-husband gets up to, but just for your knowledge, I'm almost twenty-six so fully legal and capable of making my own decisions, thank you."

My eyes flick between the two of them, waiting to see how Sarah responds. She's never really been one for confrontation, one of the reasons I never expected her to surprise Erica in the way she did. I guess it's true: women really do do crazy things for love.

"What the hell's going on?" I say, barging into the living room and making my way to the kitchen.

"Dad!" Sofia squeals, jumping from her seat and rushing over to wrap her arms around my waist.

"Hey, baby. I've got someone I'd like you to meet. This is Erica, my—"

"I know who she is. Mum's told us all about her. She's the reason you left."

Sarah retreats slightly into the corner of the room while Erica pales.

"That's not true in any way, Sof. I don't expect you to accept this straight away. I know it's hard. But Erica's a permanent part of my life now, and I think you'll really like her once you get to know her."

I glance back to Erica and hold my arm out for her. She steps up to me, but not before she swallows down her insecurities.

"Hi, Sofia. It's so nice to meet you at last."

Sarah doesn't give Sofia a chance to respond, because she steps forward.

"I'm sorry to ruin this little family bonding time, but the issue we've got right now is our daughter who's locked herself in her room, not your little plaything."

Fire burns through my veins that she has the

audacity to speak about Erica that way when she's in the same fucking room.

"That's enough. Whether you like it or not, my life is with Erica now. This isn't a fling or a midlife crisis or whatever else it is you want to call us. This is serious. We're serious."

"Bloody hell, Trey. The next thing I know, you'll be telling me she's pregnant and you're marrying her."

My anger fades slightly at her words, while Erica's hand squeezes mine.

"Oh my fucking god. She is, isn't she? You got her fucking pregnant?"

The sound of wooden chair legs scraping across the tiled floor makes the three of us wince as Sofia runs from the room.

Christ, could this get any worse?

"Well done."

"What? How was I supposed to know it was true?"

"Let me just talk to Ella, and then we'll get out of here."

"Oh great. Just storm in, cause an even bigger mess than you already have, and then run away *again*."

"We're only here because you demanded I come and sort your problem out."

"Yeah, you...not *her*."

"Enough. Sarah, I don't expect you to like it, or even accept it, but I love her, okay. And yes, we're having a baby. No, it wasn't planned or expected, but sometimes life is a little unpredictable. So can we please go and sort our daughter out so you can go out and we can leave?"

"Fine," Sarah sulks, blinking away the tears that are filling her eyes.

With one final look at Erica, who's glancing between the two of us with concern twisting her features, I follow Sarah out of the room and up the stairs.

"Ella, baby. Can you let me in please?"

"Is she still there?"

Assuming she means Sarah, I say, "Uh yeah, your mum's here."

"Ella, this is ridiculous. Just come out," Sarah snaps, clearly losing patience with our oldest daughter.

"You said you were going out. Why don't you do that?"

"I'm not leaving her here to sneak out."

"She won't. I'll make sure of it."

Sarah stares at me, I guess trying to decide if she can trust me or not, before huffing out her frustration and storming back down the stairs. I don't hear any words from downstairs, so I can only hope she ignored Erica before slamming the front door so hard the house shakes.

A few seconds after the rumble of her engine roars

on the drive, there's a click in front of me and the door opens.

Ella stands there with tears running down her face, and her chin trembles.

"Come here, baby." She slams into my chest with such force I have to take a step back.

"Thank you," she mumbles into my chest through her tears.

Guiding her over to her bed, I sit us both on the edge as she begins to calm down.

"What's going on with your mum, then?" For as long as I can remember, Ella and Sarah have clashed. Even as a baby, Ella was constantly testing her patience. It always made me wonder why she wanted another when the first one caused her so much stress.

"She's always treating me like a baby. I'm almost fifteen. I just want to do what all my friends are doing."

"And what is that exactly?"

"Loads of stuff. Going to parties, having days in town shopping, going to concerts without parents tailing along. She just makes me feel like I'm eight years old still."

"She's just being protective. You're her baby. She's finding it hard to let go." I know Sarah; at times in my life I've known her better than I've known myself, and I know exactly what she's doing here, but holding Ella back isn't going to help. She really needs to embrace that her baby is growing, and that she's responsible enough to be doing most of the things she just mentioned. If I've learnt anything from Erica, it's that you've got to try to trust people, my daughters included.

"It's so stifling, Dad. And I miss you so much. I hate this house without you in it." My heart aches, knowing that I'm playing a part in her pain right now.

"I'm so sorry. Ella...your mum said something about a boy?" I ask through gritted teeth, because as much as I think Sarah is being a little too controlling, I also hate the idea of her dating. She'll forever be too young to be spending time with boys, but I know it's something I have to accept.

Blowing out a long breath, she pulls away from me and stares at the wall. "Josh," she whispers. "He's Jade's older brother."

"I see." My insides twist. The boy my ex-wife was referring to is actually two years older than Ella. No wonder she was having a hard time with it.

"He's so sweet, Dad. He really makes me laugh and looks after me. We only wanted to go to the cinema and for some food. Nothing else was going to happen. I'm not stupid, I know what Mum's worrying about, but she needs to trust me."

"Yeah, I'm suddenly understanding why she's so worried."

"Dad," she complains. "Not you too."

I'm silent as I think about the right thing to say to her that doesn't totally undermine her mother. We were all young once and know how important things like this seemed at the time. But also, I was once a teenage boy and know exactly what my intentions were at that age when it came to girls.

"Does Jade know about you spending time with her brother?" I ask, deciding to take a different spin on it.

Ella's cheeks flush pink, giving me the answer before she says anything. "No. She hates him and his friends, she thinks they're idiots. She's right some of the time, but he's different with me. He's...sweet."

Every muscle in my body tenses. *Of course he's fucking sweet to her.* I want to stand firm and forbid her to see him but I know that won't do either of us any good. She's fast turning into a young adult and sadly, she needs to make her own mistakes and trust her own judgement.

"Ella," I say on a sigh. "I so badly want to point blank refuse to this because you're my baby and all I want to do is protect you. But I also trust you, and if you say he's sweet, I have no reason not to believe you." Her face brightens as she looks up at me with hope shining in her grey eyes. "But," her groan of frustration makes me laugh, "I also agree with your mum. You're young, and he's a teenage boy. I know you don't want to imagine it, but I was one once, and I know exactly what's going on in his head."

"Dad, it's not like—"

"I'm going to have to talk to your mum about this, but how about we set up some rules and compromise a little? Just until we get to know him."

Her teeth grind as she thinks about my offer, but I know she knows she's not going to win with me if she tries throwing another tantrum. "What does that mean exactly?"

"It means, cancel tonight. Tell him that you've got a family thing or something. Then we'll come up with a plan to do something tomorrow and you can meet him. I don't want to be that annoying, overprotective dad, but I need to meet this boy you seem so taken with."

She really doesn't want to agree, but eventually she nods. "Thanks, Dad."

"If you're up for it, there's someone I'd like you to meet downstairs."

Her face pales once again, but after a few seconds she agrees, showing me just how mature she really is despite the arguments with Sarah.

My concerns about Sofia finding out about Erica being pregnant like she did haven't left me, but as we descend the stairs, I soon realise there wasn't any need to worry.

Joyful female voices and laughter filter up to us.

"Sofia seems to like her," Ella says with a smile.

"You will too, baby. She's pretty awesome. But before we go in, I need to tell you something. Sofia already knows because you mother dropped it on her when we first arrived, but—"

"She's pregnant."

"How'd you—"

"I was eavesdropping at the top of the stairs."

"Oh, okay...well..." I stutter, not really expecting that.

"I'm really happy for you, Dad. Just like all that stuff you just said to me upstairs, I just want you to be happy too."

A ball of emotion climbs its way into my throat, blocking any words, so instead I reach out and pull my eldest daughter into my chest and hold her tight.

Things with Sarah and me might have gone south over the years, but, no matter what happens, I'll always remember she gave me two incredible daughters.

Once I feel able, I release her and look down into eyes that are so similar to mine it's almost scary. "Ready?"

"As I'll ever be."

CHAPTER FIFTEEN

"WELL THIS IS SURREAL," Erica whispers in my ear as she looks at my daughters eating their way through pizza as if they've not eaten for a week.

After a quick call to Sarah, she agreed to let us take the girls for the night. I've no idea where she'd gone, but she was a little too happy about the prospect of a child-free night so I was assuming it was a date. Fair play to her if it was—it's good to know she's trying to move on as well and stop dwelling on the fantasy that I'll return.

"Are you feeling okay?" I ask, watching her pick at her margarita pizza.

"I'm good. You're daughters are awesome. You should be so proud of them."

My chest swells that she sees exactly what I do every time I look at them.

When Ella and I rounded the corner into the living room, we found Erica and Sofia sitting on the sofa taking selfies using ridiculous Snapchat filters. Seeing them laughing together was everything to me, and the emotion that I'd just about swallowed down from Ella's words crawled its way back up.

"I am, but I'm sorry they kind of derailed our evening."

"Don't be silly. I'm enjoying myself."

"Me too, but it isn't the kind of fun I had in mind."

"Shush, they'll hear you."

"Hear what?" Sofia pipes up, making Erica's cheeks heat.

"Nothing, baby. Doesn't your mum feed you?"

"Of course."

"Leave them alone," Erica says, swatting my shoulder to stop me teasing them.

ALTHOUGH OUR EVENING WAS NICE, my girls were much quieter than they usually would be. I'm so unbelievably grateful that they seem to have accepted Erica, but I know it'll take time for it all to feel normal. Just like Sarah, they both had hopes we'd work things out eventually.

Dragging their giant bags from the boot of the car,

Erica reaches in and pulls her shopping out before we head into the building.

Going for the stairs, seeing as the lift's still got an 'out of order' sign taped to the front, I'm expecting to head all the way to the top.

"What are you doing?" I ask when Erica comes to a stop on her floor.

"I'm going to leave you guys to spend some time together. I'm exhausted. Today's been...emotional, to say the least."

The girls loiter on the steps, waiting for me to follow them. "Here, you two take the keys and let yourselves in. I'll just be a few minutes." Ella takes the keys from my outstretched hand and the two of them disappear.

As soon as I'm confident they're out of view, I step forward, crowding Erica against her door. "There were so many things I wanted to do to you tonight."

She groans in frustration, her chest rising and falling at a rapid rate.

"Your girls need you. It's fine."

I hear her voice, but the words don't register in my brain as I watch her full lips moving. Fuck, I want them on my body.

My cock swells as memories of how they feel wrapped around it fill my mind.

"Fuck," I grunt, closing the space between us and

pressing her into the wood at her back. Our bodies line up perfectly. Taking her face in my hands, I nudge my nose against hers. "Have I told you how fucking beautiful you are?"

"Trey," she whimpers, her desire for me getting the better of her. I love that she's so open about what she needs when we're together. She's never been shy of telling me exactly what to do.

"You are. So fucking beautiful. Thank you for tonight, I know it wasn't how you wanted it to go, but it means so much to me, you accepting my girls."

"They're you're daughters, Trey. I wouldn't have it any other way."

"Fuck, I love you."

My lips find hers, my tongue sliding past her lips so it can tangle with hers. The last two weeks without her have felt like a lifetime. Now she's here, beneath my hands, and I want everything she has to give, but I can't...although that doesn't mean I can't leave her wanting me just as much I as do her.

Dropping one hand from her face, I skim it down her body, circling her hard nipple when I find it pressing against the fabric of her black dress. Continuing down over her stomach, I teasingly rub between her legs over the material. She gasps, her desire making me need more.

I make quick work of finding the hem of her dress

and pushing it up around her waist, exposing her tiny lace—soaked—underwear.

"Trey, please. I need you," she breathes when I pull my lips from hers, brushing them across her jaw.

Pushing the wet fabric aside, I run my fingers through her silky folds. She's dripping for me. The temptation to fuck her right here for anyone on this floor to see is high, but picturing the two girls upstairs waiting for me, I know I can't.

"Oh god, Trey." Her head falls back against the door with a bang as I plunge two fingers deep inside her, bending them to hit the spot that has her racing towards release.

"Yes, yes, yes," she chants but, right before she falls, I pull my fingers from her body and stand back.

The sight of her heaving for breath against the door with her dress hitched up around her waist is almost my undoing.

Her dark, hungry eyes narrow on me as if she's about to kill me. "You fucking—argh," she screams, and I rush forward as the door's pulled open and she starts falling.

Thankfully, Joe's the other side and just about manages to catch her as she stumbles back into him.

"What the fuck's going—oh," he says with a laugh when he takes in the state of Erica's dress. "I thought someone was knocking, but please continue."

Stepping up to Erica, I pull her dress down, putting a stop to his roaming eyes.

"Seen it all before, mate. No need to hide it."

Fire like I've never experienced before roars in my belly and radiates out through my veins.

"You what?"

Looking between the two of us, her eyes wide in panic, Erica steps up to me, placing her palms on my chest.

"Ancient history. Put the caveman away, please." She stares into my eyes, begging me not to make a big deal about this, but the idea of any man putting their hands on what's mine makes me feel murderous. "Go inside please, Joe." Not even a second after the words leave her lips does he retreat back into their flat.

Her thumbs rub over the scruff on my cheeks as she continues looking at me. "Me and you, Trey. Me, you, those two upstairs, and this one growing in here." Dropping one hand, she takes one of mine and presses it against her stomach. "No one else matters. Not Sarah, not Joe, or anyone else from our pasts. Me and you," she repeats again just to drill the point home.

"Me and you." I nod. "You sure you don't want to come up?"

"No. I'm going straight to bed. I'll come up in the morning before we go out."

"I'll miss you."

"I'll miss you too."

With one last kiss, I take two giant steps back, forcing myself to walk away from the woman who owns me. "I love you, Erica."

She nods slightly and smiles, but she still fights saying it back. Thankfully, I can see exactly how she feels in her eyes, and it's everything I need.

By the time I get upstairs, the girls are curled up under a blanket on the sofa in their pyjamas. They've made themselves mugs of hot chocolate and have found some awful looking chick flick on Netflix. Looks like I'm in for a good night.

THE GIRLS WENT to bed over two hours ago, leaving me to thankfully turn the TV over—not that there's much I'm interested in watching. My mind is still focused on the woman beneath my feet and wondering what she might be wearing right now.

Turning the TV off, I take the glasses to the kitchen and start flicking the lights off as I head towards my bedroom when a light knock sounds out from the front door.

My heart lurches.

Turning on my heels, I reach for the door, hoping like hell that it's her. Cracking the door open, I know immediately that it is because the scent of her perfume fills my nose.

My mouth waters as I pull the door wider, getting a look at her.

"Hey, I thought you were going straight to bed."

"I did, I even fell asleep for a bit, but then I had this dream, only when I woke up, I realised it wasn't really a dream and the throbbing between my legs was very, very real."

I swallow the desire to pull her into my arms right this second in favour of hearing what else she's got to say.

"Are the girls asleep?"

"Y-yes," I stutter as she steps into the flat wearing what looks like just a long coat.

"Good." She pulls the fabric open, and my chin drops.

"Fuck me."

"That was the idea."

She's standing in my doorway in the most incredibly small set of black lace lingerie, garter belt, stockings, the whole shebang. Her bra is cupless, and the sight of her pert nipples has my knees weakening to drop to the floor and suck them into my mouth. My eyes run down over her curves and take in what I suspect is also crotchless knickers to complete the set.

"Get in here right this fucking second."

Reaching out, I grab her hand and pull her inside, making quick work of shutting and locking the door behind her.

When I turn around, she's already halfway towards my bedroom. Fuck, this woman's going to be the death of me.

I follow behind her, powerless to resist temptation and quietly close the door. I fight to drag in a breath as I stare at her standing at the end of the bed, waiting for me.

"You were saying..." I encourage, wanting to hear more about the state I left her in.

"There's this guy I know. He did this thing to me earlier."

"Oh yeah, what was that?" I ask, playing along.

"He put his hands on me. Drove me crazy. Then he walked away." Images of having her backed up against her door fill my mind, and my cock strains against the fabric of my trousers.

"Arsehole."

"My thoughts exactly."

"Hmmm...I considered using my little battery operated friend. I even thought about filming it. But, in the end, I decided it just wouldn't do."

"Why?"

"Because only one man could relieve the ache."

"Right answer, sweetheart."

Standing behind her, I take the fabric of her coat in my hands and pull it from her shoulders and down her arms.

"And what is it you need him to do exactly?"

"I need him to make me come. With his fingers, his mouth and his cock. Not necessarily in that order."

I smile, pressing my lips to the nape of her neck and kissing down the length of her spine until I hit the fabric of her thong. She's not wrong, her arousal is so strong I can smell it and my mouth waters for a taste.

"I think I'll forego the first option. Bend over, palms on the bed."

She does as I say without any hesitation or argument. The sight that greets me is fucking incredible and proves I was right about her thong being crotchless. Nudging her legs wider with my shoulders, I settle between her legs. Parting both the lace fabric and her swollen lips, I lean forward and run the tip of my tongue over the length of her. Her hips buck as she groans in frustration.

"Silence." I'd fuck her right now no matter what, but not waking the girls would be preferred. I've already put them through enough; they really don't need to listen to me making Erica scream.

Focusing my attention on her clit, I circle it until her legs are trembling and she's moaning into the duvet. Lifting my hand, I tease her entrance.

"Fucking hell," she screams into the fabric.

"Silence," I repeat, and she immediately stops. I fucking love the power she gives me like this. It's exactly what I've been craving for years.

I continue my actions, bringing her right to the edge of release before stopping and allowing the feeling to subside.

She should know by now that I won't allow her to come until I'm buried deep inside her. I'm not giving up the feeling of her squeezing down on me for fucking anything.

Sucking her clit into my mouth, I pull my fingers from inside her and lift one fingertip to her puckered arsehole. Sitting back, I watch as I circle it, my finger glistening with her arousal.

"I'm taking all of you tonight." She shudders under my touch, and I take that as her approval as she says nothing to make me think otherwise. "Stand."

She does as I say, and I sit back on my haunches and watch as she stretches her back out.

"Lie on your back."

Once again she follows orders.

"You own any more sets like this?" I ask, feasting on her lace-covered body.

"A couple. Make the most of them, because they won't fit soon."

"Oh sweetheart, you'll only look better when

you're swollen with my baby." Her thighs rub together, and I growl my disapproval. She immediately opens them, gifting me a shot of her centre.

Pulling my t-shirt over my head, I drop it to the floor with her coat, then make quick work of adding my trousers and boxers in the same pile.

Once I'm naked, my desperate cock bobbing in front of my body, I crawl onto the bed between her legs.

Leaning over her, I pull one nipple into her mouth. Her hips leave the bed as she desperately tries to find some friction to help push her over the edge, but I stay just out of reach.

Biting down on her peak, a gasp leaves her lips as she thrashes her head about.

I give the other side the same attention before licking and sucking my way up to her neck and then her ear.

"I'm going to fuck your pussy until you're begging for release. Then I'm going to finish deep in your arse."

"Yes, Trey. Now," she breathes.

"My kinky little bitch," I mutter, taking myself in my hand and rubbing the tip through her wetness, coating me in her juices ready to plunge inside her.

"Trey," she moans again.

Lifting my hand, I press my fingers to her lips to silence her.

Her eyelids flicker as I push the head of my cock inside. Her pussy ripples, trying to suck me in deeper, but I hold back, wanting her so desperate for me that the only thing she can think of is what I'm going to do next. Right now, nothing outside this bedroom exists. There's no ex-wife, no dead parents and no bullshit. It's just us.

"Just you and me," I promise as I push into her as far as she'll allow.

"Trey, fuck," she complains when I move painfully slowly, keeping her orgasm right on the edge. One wrong move and she'll crash over before I'm ready for her to.

Pulling out of her, I lean over and pull the drawer of my bedside table open. Her eyes follow me and they lock on to the little bottle of lube I pull out.

Her lips form an O as she watches me pop the top open and squeeze a generous blob onto my fingers.

"Say no if you're not up for it."

'Do it,' she mouths, finally learning her lesson about being quiet. It took fucking long enough.

Rubbing the lube around her opening, I slip one digit inside. She tenses for a second but soon relaxes once again. Pressing my thumb down on her clit, I slowly start moving my finger inside her.

"Oh shit," she groans. "Shit."

A smile twitches the edges of my lips as I watch her

try to ride me. Once she's building up to orgasm again, I slip another finger in, making her purr like a fucking kitten.

"Fuck me, Trey, fuck me."

"You sure?" I ask, not wanting to push inside her until she's good and ready.

"I'm fucking sure. I need you inside me now."

Pulling my fingers from her tight hole, I squeeze more lube on my cock and press it against her entrance.

"Oh, oh, oh," she chants as I push, trying to get past the muscle that wants to keep me out.

"Relax," I say, once again circling her clit.

She does as I say, and I push inside. Biting down on the inside of my cheeks, I fight the loud growl that wants to crawl its way up my throat. This women beneath me is so fucking incredible and so fucking mine.

Pushing in deeper, my balls almost immediately draw up, her tightness igniting my own release.

Hitting the point of no return, I press down harder on her clit. "Come," I demand, although my voice is barely a groan as I try to hold off as long as possible.

At the first clench of her orgasm hitting, I lose all fight of my own. My cock twitches violently as I fill her with everything I have.

Dropping my face to the crook of her neck, I roar out my release as she milks every last drop from me.

Collapsing on top of her, my eyelids begin to close as I enjoy the pleasure that's racing through my veins and continuing to make my muscles twitch.

"Trey?"

"Yeah?" I ask, just about managing the effort it takes to lift my head to look at her. Her eyes are tired but so soft and full of emotions.

"I love you too."

Tightening my hold on her, I place my lips to hers and kiss her as if it's the last thing I'll ever do while my heart threatens to explode in my chest.

CHAPTER SIXTEEN

IT SEEMS to be becoming normal that when I wake up in the morning that I'm alone, the other side of the bed cold, almost as if her body lying beside mine was all a dream.

Sitting myself on the edge, I wipe my tired eyes and head towards the en suite, assuming it's where she'll be.

The small room is in darkness when I get there, and flicking on the light confirms what I suspect. Turning, I rush back into the room hoping to find her elsewhere in the flat but already guessing that she's escaped home. I can only hope that doesn't mean she's regretting everything that's happened between us in the last few days...or agreeing to the house. My mind flicks back to walking around the new house with her yesterday. Even from the moment we stepped through the front door, it felt like home.

I spot the note on the bed as soon as I step out of the en suite.

> *I've gone downstairs to get ready.*
> *Come and get me when you're ready to go out.*
> *I love you.*
> *E xx*

Those three words make my heart pound violently in my chest, making me want to storm straight downstairs and claim her as mine once again. I'm not sure this all-consuming need for her is ever going to abate. No matter how many times I have her, it's never enough.

Giggling from outside my door is a sobering reminder that I can't do exactly what I want right now. I've got two other people to worry about first.

Pulling on some clothes, I head out to meet my girls.

"Morning, did you both sleep okay?"

"Yeah, thanks, Dad."

"Ella's been awake hours. She's excited," Sofia sings, much to Ella's mortification.

"No, I'm not. My body just knew I was somewhere different and woke me up earlier than usual."

"Whatever." Sofia rolls her eyes at her sister and turns to me. "What's for breakfast?"

"You know you're going to like a boy one day and I'm going to get my own back."

"Ugh, I doubt it. Boys are gross."

"That's what they all say," Ella says while staring into her phone, a smile appearing on her face.

I try not to think about what—or who—is making her so happy. I want her to have the same opinion about boys as Sofia. I'm not ready for this.

"Okay so, we've got...toast or cereal."

"Wow, exciting."

"I'd offer to take you out, but we're already going out for lunch so..."

"Toast is great, Dad. Thanks."

Knowing she's downstairs and waiting for us means every minute ticks by at a snail's pace.

"What time have you agreed to meet Josh?" I just about manage to get his name out through gritted teeth.

"Eleven-thirty outside Costa. Our film starts at midday."

"Okay. I'm going to shower and dress. Do either of you need anything?"

"No, we're good. I'm going to come and get ready too."

"I look over at my eldest daughter who's currently still wearing her pyjamas. "Ella?"

"Yeah?"

"Can you do me a favour?"

"Sure, what is it?"

"Make sure you're suitably covered up for this...this afternoon. I'm doing you a massive favour allowing it to happen, so it's for the best that you don't push your luck."

"I wasn't planning on going dressed like a hooker, don't worry."

I open my mouth to respond, but no words come out. Instead I just stand there, watching her skip off to the room she shared with her sister last night.

"She's growing up so fast," Sofia says, clearly watching our interaction.

"Smart arse," I mutter, heading off to my own bedroom and leaving her with her tablet to keep her entertained.

It takes Ella forever to get ready.

"I'm going to go and get her. She'll miss the whole thing if she doesn't hurry up."

She runs off down the hallway, leaving me with my own anticipation about today. I hate what I'm allowing Ella to do, but I know it's the right thing. I don't want to stop her growing up, no matter how much I might hate it. But I need to know she's going to be okay, and I want to meet Josh. Not to give him 'the dad speech' but just so I can look him in the eye and get a sense for the kind of boy he is. I just pray that he's someone I'm going to be able to trust. If he looks like a scumbag, I've no issue with dragging Ella back out the way we came and locking her inside her bedroom for the next ten years.

When she eventually emerges and I glance over, a lump forms in my throat. She's so beautiful and looks way older than her almost fifteen years. Her hair is hanging straight around her shoulders, she's got dark but minimal make-up around her eyes, and pinker than usual lips, but it's her outfit of choice that makes my heart swell. I expected her to attempt to get out of this house wearing the shortest skirt she could get away with, but in reality she's standing in front of me in a pair of grey skinny jeans and a black t-shirt sporting a band's name that I've never heard of.

"What? Why are you looking at me like that?"

"I'm just wondering how I helped make something so beautiful."

"Aw, you getting all soppy, old man?"

"Enough of that, please."

"You're right, we should stop referencing your age just in case Erica realises her mistake and dumps you."

"You cheeky little—"

I reach for her to pull her in for a hug, but she side steps me and goes for her jacket and then the door instead.

"Come on, we're going to be late."

"And whose fault would that be?" I call after her with a laugh. Sofia and I both grab our own coats before following her out of the flat to go and get Erica.

Ella's waiting beside the door when we both step onto her floor. "You said you met her at work. How come she lives in the same building?"

"Total coincidence." Her brows draw together. "I'm serious. I had no idea for weeks."

"That's weird but hilarious."

Shaking my head at my daughter, I lift my hand to knock. The door opens almost immediately, but instead of Erica appearing, it's Joe.

"Hey, is she ready?" The moment my eyes land on him, I'm reminded of the comment he made yesterday about being intimate with Erica, and the fire it started in my belly reignites.

"She's in the toilet. I just wanted to apologise for last night. What I said was thoughtless, and you were right to be pis—angry," he corrects when he spots my girls behind me. "It was a long time ago and..." he pauses, his face twisting in uncertainty. "Anyway, what have you got planned for Thursday?" His voice is barely a whisper, forcing me to lean in a little to hear him.

"What's Thursday?"

Rolling his eyes, he tuts. "Erica's birthday of course," he says as if it should be obvious.

My stomach drops. "Shit, I had no idea."

"There's still time to pull it out of the bag, but with the number of times she throws up every morning, I'd suggest you do something seriously special."

"What are you two whispering about?" Erica asks as she walks our way.

"Just naughty things we don't want the kids to hear."

"Jesus, Joe. Do you ever stop talking about S-E-X?"

"We can spell," Ella calls with a laugh.

"Fuck."

"We know what that means too."

Joe snorts out a laugh while Erica looks like she's waiting for the ground to swallow her up.

"You still sure about me being a mother?"

"Most definitely. Just ignore them, they're too smart for their own good."

I don't need to turn around to know they're probably sticking their tongues out at me or something equally as stupid. Erica's amusement gives them away.

"Are you ready to go?"

"Yes. Let me grab my bag and we'll get this date on the road."

"Don't remind me."

Ella is silent as we drive towards the shopping centre where we're meeting Josh. I've agreed to allow them to go to the cinema and then to get some food after while Erica, Sofia and I have lunch ourselves and do some shopping. I feel better knowing we'll at least be close should she need me, which I know she won't.

"It's sweet how nervous she is," Erica whispers as we follow the girls towards the shops. "I remember being that excited. Young love is so sweet."

"I don't know. Old love is pretty awesome too."

"Old! Speak for yourself. I've got a few years until I can be considered old yet, thank you very much."

As we round the corner, heading towards Costa, there's a floppy-haired teenage boy loitering outside. Glancing over at Ella, I notice her shoulders are pulled tight as she fiddles nervously with a lock of her hair.

"Is that him?" I whisper in her ear.

"Yeah. Dad, please don't embarrass me."

"I promise. I just want to meet him."

Erica, Sofia and I hang back as she walks up to him. The second he sees her, the widest smile spreads across his face and his eyes go all soft. It's everything I needed to see.

His smile turns goofy as she steps up to him and they greet each other.

"Oh my god, they are so cute," Erica coos beside me. "I think he might be a good one."

"I hate to admit it, but me too."

Ella hesitantly turns to us, and I step forward. "This is my dad and his...girlfriend." She hesitates to introduce Erica that way, and I understand why.

"Josh, nice to meet you," I greet with a curt nod of my head. I might have had good first impressions, but I'm not allowing him to see that I might approve of him spending time with my baby.

"Mr. Bennett, it's so nice to meet you. Ella always talks about you."

"Really?" I ask, looking at my daughter, who's trying to hide behind him in embarrassment. "And it's Trey. Mr. Bennett makes me sound old." Erica stifles a laugh behind me that ensures she's in for a long night once we drop the girls back at home.

"So...now that's all out of the way, we're gonna go," Ella points over her shoulder. "We'll meet you back here at four, yeah?"

"Yeah just—"

"Keep my phone on just in case. Yeah, I know. We're good, right?" She glances at Josh who just looks between the two of us with slight panic in his eyes.

"Yeah. It was nice to meet you. I promise to get her back on time."

"I should hope so. Be good." Ella fumes at my words and turns to storm off.

"Did you have to do that?" Erica chastises.

"Couldn't help myself. He needs to know who he's going to answer to if he fucks this up."

"Just give him a chance. He could be your future son-in-law."

"Fucking hell," I mutter, stepping forward into the crowds. "Where to first?"

I spend most of the day following Erica and Sofia around the shops. They do a good job of trying to keep me distracted, but I can't help worrying about Ella and wondering what she's doing and if Josh is behaving.

We walk towards Costa a few minutes before four o'clock. I'm expecting to have to wait for them but, to my shock, both Ella and Josh are standing outside with a takeaway cup in hand.

"Wow, I'm impressed." Ella blushes while Josh looks pleased with himself. "Okay, well...we'll just wait over here while you say goodbye. No tongues though, please. I'm not sure my heart could cope with that."

IF THE SILENCE in the car as we drive towards my old house tells me anything, it's that everyone feels the same about going back there. There's a high chance that Ella and Sarah will probably end up in another argument; I could tell by her tone on the phone when I told her what I was going to do that she wasn't happy about it, and Sofia will be left to listen to them shouting at each other.

I know they both love Sarah—she's their mum and she's good at it—but I still hate dropping them off every time I get to spend decent time with them. I miss them so much.

Erica and I say our goodbyes and see them both into the house from the car. I've no intention of getting an ear-bashing from my ex-wife for what we did today. I'll stand by my decision to allow Ella and Josh to spend time together, once she's really thought about it she'll know I was right.

"You'll see them again next weekend, right?"

"I guess. It's just not the same as seeing them every day."

"I can't imagine how that must feel. I've only known about this one a few weeks, but already I feel weirdly attached. I can't imagine going any amount of time without him—sorry," she says with a wince when she sees the pain on my face. "What can I do to distract you?"

"I've got a few ideas. I might even let you scream tonight."

"Good to know. Take me home then."

The drive is tense and hurried. Both of us know what's going to happen the second we're behind closed doors, and both of us are desperate for it to begin.

I pull the car to a stop haphazardly in my parking space, not giving two shits as to whether it's within the lines or not, and jump out. Erica's already halfway out when I get around to her. Not wanting to wait for her, I grab her around the waist and lift her over my shoulder.

"Trey, put me down," she squeals but soon stops when I slap her arse.

With her securely in place, I jog up the stairs to her flat.

"Keys," I demand and take her bag from her when she offers it to me. Stuffing my hand all the way to the bottom, I eventually wrap my fingers around her giant fluffy keyring and tug.

I've got the door open in mere seconds and we're pushing our way in. I'm intending on walking straight down to her room, but the moment I look up towards her door, my body freezes finding someone—or two people—in our way.

"Trey, what the hell?"

It's only when Erica's voice fills the room that the

bodies in front of us still before looking our way, total horror covering their faces.

"What's going o—oooh!" Erica giggles as I lower her feet to the floor and her eyes also land on a half-naked Joe with his hips pinning a petite dark, haired-woman to the wall. Although her dress is hitched up around her waist, it just about covers her dignity, but it's pretty obvious what's going on right now.

"Fuck. I thought you said it would be safe."

"I didn't think...fuck. Some privacy?"

"Yeah, shit. Sorry. Let's go to your place."

Both of us back up. I turn to head towards the door, but Erica keeps her eyes on Joe, some kind of silent conversation passing between them before she eventually turns her back on them and we both head up to my flat.

"Who was that?"

"I've no idea, but I'd put fucking money on the fact she has something to do with whatever he does every Thursday night."

"Oh?" I ask, intrigued as to what Joe's up to.

"I've no idea what he's doing. He's been really evasive about it, and I don't like it. He's made some really fucked up decisions in the past, so I wish he'd talk about whatever this one is."

"I'm sure he will when he's ready," I say, shutting

the door behind me and nuzzling my nose into her neck, breathing in her scent.

"I guess."

"Now, stop worrying about him and start worrying about your boyfriend."

"Boyfriend?" Her eyebrows rise in delight where as my stomach drops slightly at just being her boyfriend. That's not enough for me. She's carrying my baby, and we're about to buy our first house together. I want more.

CHAPTER SEVENTEEN

AS DESPERATE AS I was to do something totally over-the-top for Erica's birthday, I knew she wouldn't thank me for it. She's not that kind of girl. So in the end I went with something a little more low key that I knew she'd love.

She won't admit it, but I know she's feeling a little lost since losing her mother. They may not have had a relationship aside from Sunday morning visits where her mum was only usually present in body but still, losing a parent is huge, even if they weren't really there in the first place.

Her pregnancy might have been a total shock, but looking at it now, I think it's the best thing that could have happened. It's given her something to focus on. Her mum's gone and Sam's busy embarking on married life. It's time to show her that what she might be lacking in actual family she makes up for with others in her life.

It took some serious string pulling and sweet talking, but I manage to book a table at my favourite restaurant for tonight. I thought the vein in Mark's temple was going to explode when I turned up demanding a setting for eight at four days' notice in a restaurant that's booked out months in advance. Thankfully, knowing the chef and spending countless amounts of money here in the past meant I secured the table.

Erica has no idea what the plan was for tonight. It wasn't easy seeing as she returned to work on Monday and started nagging Lauren for answers about what I was planning, but thankfully, Lauren kept her lips sealed. The only thing she knew was that a taxi would be waiting for her about twenty minutes ago and that she was to just go with the flow—not something I'm expecting her to be all that happy about. She might tell me now that she trusts me, but I'm fully aware that in reality she probably never fully will, and that's okay. She's had her trust smashed by people time and time again. The fact that she trusts me as much as she does after what I did to her is a blessing. She would have been well within her rights to never talk to me again. I guess I once again need to thank that surprise little person growing in her belly. I've no idea what would have happened if he wasn't there.

"Is she here yet?" Lauren asks, rubbing her palms on her thighs nervously.

"Don't think so. Why are you nervous? It's not like we're going to turn the lights out and scare the crap out of her."

"I know. I'm just excited for her to see what you've done. She probably expects to just find you waiting for her."

"I haven't really done anything. It's just a meal with friends and a few balloons."

"It's more than that and you know it. You've brought her family together when she needs it most. Don't think I can't see exactly what your plan was, Trey. And also don't think that I don't see she's struggling. I failed her once before by not noticing what was going on with her, I made her a promise it wouldn't happen again."

"I know, and so does she. It's exactly why you're here right now."

"Where the hell's Joe?"

"It's a Thursday night, who knows."

"He still hasn't said anything?"

"Nope, just that he'd be here as soon as he could."

"I need to have words with that boy," Lauren

warns, clearly as concerned as Erica is about what he's up to. "Oh, oh there she is."

Lifting my eyes to Mark at the maître de stand, I find her immediately, wearing a loose-fitting shift dress that shows off her incredibly shapely legs.

"Don't even think about getting your hands up there in this fancy restaurant, Mr. Bennett," Lauren growls quietly, reminding me what happened on our last group outing.

"I'll do my best, but at times they have a mind of their own."

"Don't I know it," she mutters before falling silent when Erica looks directly at me. I don't think she even sees the others surrounding me.

To begin with, concern fills her eyes. I'm not surprised: this is the exact place where her world exploded in front of her, but as far as I'm concerned, it still has the best food in the city and I want her to experience it and hopefully to overwrite her previous memory of the place.

Eventually, she takes a step towards me. Pushing out the chair behind me, I stand and hold my hand out for her.

"I have to say, I'm glad you're here first this time."

"We wanted to surprise you."

"We?" It's only then when she looks down to her right and finds everyone looking up at her. "Oh my god." Her eyes land on everyone around the table. Lauren, Ben, their friend Danni—which I've discovered was where Erica was hiding after her first visit here—Ella and Sofia, then finally an empty chair.

"Joe said he'd be here as soon as he could."

Shaking her head, she plasters on a smile, trying to hide her concern. "I can't believe you did this. Thank you so much."

"Happy birthday, sweetheart."

We both take our seats before I pick up the small square box I placed on the table when we first arrived. I hand it to Erica.

"What's this?"

"Your birthday present. What does it look like?" No one else knows what's in the box and all of their eyes soon zero in on it as Erica removes the wrapping. I know exactly what they're all thinking, and I hope they're not too disappointed. They don't know her like I do, and as much as I want it to be what they're hoping for, I know she's not ready. Lauren's eyes bore into me; I can practically hear her screaming that I should be on one knee.

Her hands tremble as she flips the lid open, and I hope that's a sign that I did the right thing. She gasps. "Oh, they're gorgeous. Thank you so much."

"You're more than welcome." Reaching out, I wrap my hand around the back of her neck and pull her lips to mine. Our kiss is much more reserved than I want to give her, but knowing everyone around the table is watching, including my daughters, stops me from shoving my tongue deep in her mouth.

"I love you, sweetheart. Happy birthday."

"I love you too. Thank you."

The waiter interrupts our moment to take our drinks orders. When Erica's distracted, Lauren leans over.

"What the hell? Where's the ring?" she hisses. The day my solicitor rang to tell me that Sarah had at last signed the papers, I took Lauren out on a little shopping trip to help me find the right one. She begged the entire day to find out what I was planning, but I refused to say anything.

"It's coming. Have a little patience." Her lips purse in frustration, but she sits back nonetheless.

Sitting back, I silently take in Erica chatting with her friends and trying to drag Ella and Sofia into whatever it is they're talking about, and I wonder how I ended up here. There was a time not so long ago that I thought I was destined to be stuck in a life I wasn't happy with, but then just when I needed her most, there she was, like a guardian fucking angel. She has no idea, but she saved me. She saw the man I was desperate to become and she allowed me to be myself. I'll never forget everything she's given me.

EPILOGUE

Erica

WHEN I HELD that little black box in my hand the night of my birthday, I'd have put money on it being an engagement ring. I thought I would have been scared— terrified actually—but in reality it just felt right. Things hadn't been easy since meeting Trey, but even with everything, I wouldn't want anyone else beside me for the journey we're about to embark on.

When I opened the box, I found a stunning set of diamond earrings staring back at me. They were gorgeous, don't get me wrong, but my heart dropped a little. Neither of us had talked about marriage; we were too tied up with my surprise pregnancy and the house. I had no idea if Trey even wanted to get married again but, without realising it, I'd been hoping for it. From the disappointment on everyone's faces around me, I'm pretty sure they were expecting it too.

I've never been one to dream about my wedding, my dress and what the colour scheme might be. I was too focused on getting through life without meeting another arsehole who was intent on ruining it. But the second that non-engagement box was placed in my hands, it was suddenly all I could think about. I took that as a very good sign. It was telling me that he was the one and that I was ready to jump in with both feet. From that moment, everything seemed a little less scary. My worry about being a mother waned a little, although that was never going to disappear entirely. I stopped second-guessing the house and just tried to enjoy our second chance.

Knowing how happy he makes me, I can't help feeling stupid for running away when I discovered his secret, but if I've learnt anything about life, it's that living in the past is pointless. It's always better to focus on right now and the future, the things you can change and make better.

And that's exactly why, every time something big comes like Christmas and then New Year, I expect that little box to appear.

But it never does.

We spent Christmas with Ben and Lauren. They'd booked a huge, gorgeous house in the Cotswolds for the entire holiday. It was probably one of my best Christmases, surrounded by people I love. The only people who were missing were Sam, who spent the festive season with Cliff's family, and Ella and Sofia, but they came to us for New Year.

I'd never expressed my desire to feel the weight of Trey's ring on my finger, but every time Lauren looked at me, I knew she could feel it. I waved her off every time. If Trey wasn't asking, he had a very good reason, and I had to trust him. I also made a point not to ask, afraid of coming off like I was demanding to tie him down because really, I wasn't.

I just wanted everything and to have the same surname as our baby.

"Are you ready?"

"Nearly. You know the appointment isn't until eleven, right?" I ask, glancing at the clock, seeing that it's not even nine."

"I don't want to be late. There might be traffic."

Chuckling at his excitement, I grab my coat and head out into the kitchen of my flat to find him. After we discovered Joe and his mystery woman in the hallway, it was agreed by all that maybe it was time to rethink our living arrangements, so Trey moved down here with me and Joe moved up to his flat. It was the perfect solution as it allowed us to live as a couple and gave Joe his freedom to do his own thing without worrying about getting caught. I still remember the horror on his girl's face that night.

"What the hell are you going to be like as my due date approaches?" I ask after Trey pulls me in for a kiss.

"Ready. I'll be ready."

"I guess it could be worse," I mutter lightly.

"Come on, I want to see our boy."

"You know it might not actually be a boy, right?"

"Of course."

Hand in hand, we head out of the flat to find his car, avoiding the boxes littering the hallway. We're meant to get the keys to our new house on Friday. I thought I'd be sad to leave this place, but knowing that house with all its space is waiting for me, I'm a little less concerned about the whole thing.

Trey's knee bounces the entire time we're sitting in the waiting room. I know I found out about my pregnancy a little later than most women probably do, but now I'm sitting here waiting to see my baby for the first time, it feels like the weeks have just flown by, which is a little odd seeing as almost everything about my life has changed in that time.

"Miss Wilde, please."

My heart jumps up into my throat knowing that it's my turn. Trey reaches out and takes my trembling hand as he leads me towards the sonographer.

"You okay?"

"Yeah, I'm excited."

"Me too, sweetheart." Leaning over, he places a sweet kiss to my temple and my eyelids shutter closed for a second.

I hop up on the bed and do everything I'm told while my heart threatens to pound out of my chest. Adrenaline is buzzing around my body so much that I don't even flinch when the gel is squirted on my body like I always see on TV.

"Okay, are you both ready?"

"Yes."

With that, the sonographer presses a white wand thing into my belly and stares at the screen. She wiggles it about a little while her focus stays on whatever is in front of her. Tears burn my eyes that I can't see my baby and she can, but only a couple of seconds later, she turns the screen.

I gasp, my hand coming up to cover my mouth as Trey squeezes my other. There on the screen is a perfect black and white picture of a baby. He must be lying just right, because I can make out every bit of his body.

"Oh my god," I sob.

"I need to take a couple more measurements, but everything's looking good. Would you like me to print pictures?"

"Y-yes please."

Her words barely register as I continue to stare at the screen through tear-filled eyes.

"That's our baby," I whisper in total amazement.

"It is." The sound of Trey's choked voice is just about enough to drag my eyes away from the screen, and I'm so bloody glad I do because the look of awe and amazement on his face as he stares at our little person is the most incredible sight I think I've ever seen.

"That's our baby," he confirms, turning his equally damp eyes on mine. "I love you so much."

"I love you too."

The rest of the time with the sonographer rubbing the wand across my belly is a total daze. Before I know it, we're done and Trey is paying for our photos and we're left alone with the images of our baby so I can clean up.

"That was incredible," I say as I swing my legs from the bed, dropping the goo covered tissue into the bin beside it.

Standing, I pull my leggings up and am just about to right my top when movement at the end of the bed catches my eye.

"Trey, what are you—uh," I gasp once again when he slowly drops to one knee.

"I can't wait any longer." He reaches out a hand for me, and I step forward, although my brain doesn't register the movement. "Erica, I've been holding off until I thought you were ready, but I'm done waiting. I want to make you mine officially. When I'm with you, I'm the man I've always wanted to be. You make me a better person, and I can't imagine the rest of my life without you in it. Erica Wilde, will you marry me?"

A sob erupts before I manage to form any words. The tears that were still in my eyes from seeing our baby spill over and drop to my cheeks. "Yes, Trey. Yes," I whisper. What I really want to do is scream it from the rooftops, but the emotion blocking my throat stops me.

Reaching into his coat pocket, he pulls out a familiar little black box.

"I hope there's no earrings inside that," I say with a laugh.

"Not this time, sweetheart."

He opens the box and my eyes almost pop out of my head. "It's huge."

His lips press into a thin line as he fights not to make a joke in what should be a serious situation. "Only the best for my fiancée."

He plucks the giant solitaire diamond from its cushioning and slides it up my trembling finger.

"I knew you were different the moment I saw you sitting at the bar that night. I never could have imagined how much you'd change my life."

Dragging my eyes up from admiring my new piece of jewellery, I drink in the love that's pouring from his eyes and I know without a doubt that the disasters of my past were only there so that one day it would lead me to Trey. Stepping forward, I reach up and press my lips to his. "I love you."

"I love you, too. And our little nugget," he says, placing his hands on my belly. "I can't wait for what's to come."

Are you ready for Joe's story? Avoiding Temptation is
NOW LIVE
DOWNLOAD NOW

ACKNOWLEDGMENTS

Erica and Trey orginially weren't going to have a book. I was intending on going in a totally different direction, but I'm glad they screamed so loud. I've loved writing this intense duet and experiencing them fall for each other not only in the first book but even harder for each other in this second. It's been a bit of a bumpy ride for them both, but they got there in the end.

And that baby...what do you think—boy or girl? I'm hoping we find out in the next duet in the series.

As always, I've got a huge list of people to thank for helping and supporting me with this book. Michelle, as always, for being an epic alpha reader and telling me exactly how it is. Deanna, Lindsay, Susanne and Tracy, for patiently waiting for the second installment of Erica and Trey's story and not sending me too much abuse for it. I was feeling the pressure after writing Ben, but you reassured me that Trey stood up...and maybe even overtook him at times.

Samantha, you've been a life saver with everything you've been doing. I'm not sure how I ever coped without you!

Evelyn, again, for putting up with me and my incredibly repetitive typos. One day I might spot them myself—we can only hope!

Paige, for proofreading and making this as perfect as possible.

And, last but never least, my long-suffering husband and daughter for putting up with my crazy arse. I love you x

ABOUT THE AUTHOR

Tracy Lorraine is a *USA Today* and *Wall Street Journal* bestselling new adult and contemporary romance author. Tracy has recently turned thirty and lives in a cute Cotswold village in England with her husband, baby girl and lovable but slightly crazy dog. Having always been a bookaholic with her head stuck in her Kindle, Tracy decided to try her hand at a story idea she dreamt up and hasn't looked back since.

Be the first to find out about new releases and offers. Sign up to my newsletter here.

If you want to know what I'm up to and see teasers and snippets of what I'm working on, then you need to be in my Facebook group. Join Tracy's Angels here.

Keep up to date with Tracy's books at
www.tracylorraine.com

Falling Series

Falling for Ryan: Part One #1

Falling for Ryan: Part Two #2

Falling for Jax #3

Falling for Daniel (A Falling Series Novella)

Falling for Ruben #4

Falling for Fin #5

Falling for Lucas #6

Falling for Caleb #7

Falling for Declan #8

Falling For Liam #9

Forbidden Series

Falling for the Forbidden #1

Losing the Forbidden #2

Fighting for the Forbidden #3

Craving Redemption #4

Demanding Redemption #5

Avoiding Temptation #6

<u>Chasing Temptation</u> #7

<u>Rebel Ink Series</u>

<u>Hate You</u> #1

<u>Trick You</u> #2

<u>Defy You</u> #3

<u>Play You</u> #4

<u>Inked</u> (A Rebel Ink/Driven Crossover)

<u>Rosewood High Series</u>

<u>Thorn</u> #1

<u>Paine</u> #2

<u>Savage</u> #3

<u>Fierce</u> #4

<u>Hunter</u> #5

Faze (#6 Prequel)

<u>Fury</u> #6

<u>Legend</u> #7

<u>Maddison Kings University Series</u>

<u>TMYM: Prequel</u>

<u>TRYS #1</u>

<u>TDYW #2</u>

<u>TBYS</u> #3

<u>TVYC</u> #4

<u>TDYD</u> #5

<u>TDYR</u> #6

<u>TRYD</u> #7

<u>Knight's Ridge Empire Series</u>

<u>Wicked Summer Knight</u>: Prequel (Stella & Seb)

<u>Wicked Knight</u> #1 (Stella & Seb)

<u>Wicked Princess</u> #2 (Stella & Seb)

<u>Wicked Empire</u> #3 (Stella & Seb)

<u>Deviant Knight</u> #4 (Emmie & Theo)

<u>Deviant Princess</u> #5 (Emmie & Theo

<u>Deviant Reign</u> #6 (Emmie & Theo)

<u>One Reckless Knight</u> (Jodie & Toby)

<u>Reckless Knight</u> #7 (Jodie & Toby)

<u>Reckless Princess</u> #8 (Jodie & Toby)

<u>Reckless Dynasty</u> #9 (Jodie & Toby)

<u>Dark Halloween Knight</u> (Calli & Batman)

<u>Dark Knight</u> #10 (Calli & Batman)

<u>Dark Princess</u> #11 (Calli & Batman)

Dark Legacy #12 (Calli & Batman)

<u>Corrupt Valentine Knight</u> (Nico & Siren)

<u>Ruined Series</u>

<u>Ruined Plans</u> #1

<u>Ruined by Lies</u> #2

<u>Ruined Promises</u> #3

<u>Never Forget Series</u>

<u>Never Forget Him</u> #1

<u>Never Forget Us</u> #2

<u>Everywhere & Nowhere</u> #3

<u>Chasing Series</u>

<u>Chasing Logan</u>

<u>The Cocktail Girls</u>

<u>His Manhattan</u>

<u>Her Kensington</u>

FALLING FOR THE FORBIDDEN
SNEAK PEEK
CHAPTER ONE

Falling down on my bed, I blow out a long breath and tell myself that everything will be okay.

I had plans for this summer—a few weeks of fun before uni starts. The girls and I had been looking at last-minute holiday deals, and we had tickets for a music festival...but then my dad swooped in, in that way that he does, and ruined everything.

I knew it was coming.

I just wasn't expecting it quite yet.

I'd hoped agreeing to study what he wanted me to and working for him was enough—apparently not.

I decided a few years ago that I wasn't going to move away to study. I mostly love my life in London, and I loved living with Mum. I'm not ashamed to admit that she's one of my best friends. It was only as I started looking at universities that my dad piped up and told me that I would be studying accountancy and finance at The London School of Economics. He'd done his research and decided it was the best place for me to learn my trade so I could enter the family business.

I just about managed to contain my laughter when he emphasised the word *family*.

I've no idea how long I lie on my bed trying to convince myself that moving into his house with his new wife and her son isn't the worst thing to ever happen to me, but eventually my stomach rumbling has me moving. I sit on the edge of the bed and take in all my half-unpacked boxes. A large sigh falls from my lips. If I don't find everything a home, maybe I won't have to stay. I know it's wishful thinking. This is it for me now.

Disappointment floods me as I make my way through the silent house. It's not that I was expecting a welcome party or anything, but someone being here would have been nice. Someone to help me carry everything up to my room would have been even nicer. Since Dad moved in with Jenny a few years ago, I've been told to treat this place like my home.

It will never be.

It's just a house, a show home, a shell in which I'm scared to touch anything for fear of making a mess. Home is a place with character, with mess from day-to-day living, with people who love and care for you.

My dad isn't a bad man, per se, but he's not exactly what you'd describe as a doting father. Everything he does is for his own gain—if it happens to help others in the process, that's just a bonus.

My step mum, Jenny, is lovely. She really is, but I can't help feeling like she's just a little bit...broken. She makes all the right comments and does all the right things. She's a great mum. But there's such sadness in her eyes.

The fridge is full, as usual. It's strange, because I've never witnessed anyone eating more than a slice of toast or an apple in this kitchen.

I fix myself a salad with the unopened packets of fruit and vegetables, but it doesn't really have the effect I needed it to have. Being here makes me feel kind of empty, and no amount of lettuce leaves is going to fill the void after moving out of the flat Mum and I shared for the past few years.

Rummaging through the cupboards, I can't help smiling when I find a stash of naughty stuff hiding at the back.

Pulling my hair back into a messy bun, I put my thoughts to the side and set about making something that will make me feel just a little bit better.

The sun's just about to set, casting an orange glow throughout the kitchen. It almost makes it feel warm and inviting—almost. My mouth waters as I pour melted chocolate over the crushed biscuits and marshmallows I've managed not to eat already. Standing in only a vest and a small pair of hot pants, I decide to make myself a hot chocolate, grab a blanket, and enjoy my bowl of goodness out on the deck with a magazine. Chocolate makes everything that little bit better. If I eat enough, it might make me forget what this summer's actually going to be like for me.

I'm just waiting for the kettle to boil when a shiver runs down my spine. I'm sure it's just the size of the house that freaks me out. I've seen enough horror films to know there are plenty of hiding places in a place this big.

I'm still for a second, but when I don't hear anything, I continue with what I was doing. That is, until a deep rumbling voice has every nerve in my body on alert.

"Wow, step daddy sure is attracting the young ones these days." His voice is slurred, his anger palpable. It makes goosebumps prick my skin and a giant lump form in my throat. "You look too pure. Too innocent to be with that prick," he spits.

There's no love lost between my dad and my stepbrother, that's not news to me, but the viciousness of his voice right now makes me wonder what their relationship is really like. My dad might be many things, but he wouldn't cheat on Jenny—he loves her too much.

I can't remember the last time I saw him, but there's no way he can't know it's me. Who the hell else would be cooking in his kitchen? Deciding he's just trying to rile me up, I go to collect my stuff and get out of his way. Unfortunately, he seems to have other ideas.

His breath tickles up my neck moments before the heat of his body warms my back.

"You came here for the wrong man. I can put that right, though." The alcohol on his breath surrounds me. It's a reminder that there's a good chance he has no idea what he's doing right now.

The softness of his nose running up the length of my neck has tingles racing through my traitorous body. I don't realise he's smelling me until he blows out a long breath and the scent of alcohol hits me once again. I turn to leave, but his hands slam on the counter behind me and cage me in.

"Look at me," he demands.

"Let me go, Ben."

If he's surprised to discover it's me, he doesn't show it. If anything, his eyes shine with delight as he takes in every inch of my face before focusing on my lips. My stomach flips, knowing where his thoughts are.

Something passes over his face but it's gone too quickly to be able to identify. He pushes himself from the counter and away from me. No more words are said, but when he gets to the door, he looks back over his shoulder and runs his eyes over my body. They hold a warning I don't really understand.

Once he's disappeared from sight, I sag back against the counter. What the hell was that?

After putting half of the rocky road on a tray in the fridge, I forgo sitting outside and instead take my spoils to my room to hide. There's stuff everywhere in my room and, unlike the rest of this house, it makes me feel a little more relaxed.

Since the day Ben and I were introduced by our parents, we've not really had any kind of relationship. He's pretty much stayed out of my way and, in turn, I've done the same. It's not all that much of a task. When I'm here, he spends almost every minute somewhere else. When he's home, he's moody, arrogant, and generally a prick, so I'm more than happy to stay out of his way.

It's just a shame he's so damn pretty to look at. As the years have passed, he's only become more attractive, too. I've no idea if it's just his job or if he works out as well because every inch of him seems to be toned to perfection.

Jenny spends most of her time apologising for his attitude and trying to explain that he's got a lot going on. I'm yet to discover what that is. As far as I can tell, he seems to be your average twenty-year-old guy who'd rather be off his arse drunk or with a woman than spending time at home with his parents.

By the time I've dug my way to the bottom of the bowl, I feel pretty sick. There's still no sign of my dad or Jenny, but the music pounding from Ben's room across the hallway leaves no doubt as to what kind of mood he's in.

DOWNLOAD NOW to continue Lauren and Ben's story.